TRUCKIN' TO PLEASE

TRUCKIN' TO PLEASE

JERRY RABUSHKA

QUEERMOJO
A Rebel Satori Imprint
New Orleans

Published in the United States of America by
Queer Mojo
A Rebel Satori Imprint
www.rebelsatoripress.com

Edited by Jerry L. Wheeler

Paperback ISBN: 978-1-60864-208-3
Ebook ISBN: 978-1-60864-209-0
Library of Congress Control Number: 2022940705

CONTENTS

To Cherry

CHAPTER I

Morgan's Diner, 2:00 A.M., Manchester Road, Maplewood, Missouri. Spring, 1991.

Castor sits at the back of the counter staring into a nearly empty plate of fries, his head leaning on his hand, eyes moving back and forth between the guys at the video game and the swirls of ketchup left over in his plate. He thinks about going home, thinks about staying here. Sometimes he doesn't think at all.

Just got done driving the eighteen-wheeler from the west of Kansas. West of Wyoming, west of Nebraska. Odd, because he's hardly driven out there before. Just taking someone's place who couldn't make the trip. Somehow Morgan's Diner seemed like the right speed for him. As dead a society as he could find at this hour.

He pulled his '58 Ford into his driveway and didn't feel like going in the house. Nothing there but a sick mother and some furniture as old as the Ford. But he's proud of the Ford. His family bought it new.

He's still a little hypnotized from the road. That's how he likes it. Trudged a few blocks from Bleeck Avenue up to Manchester, real slow like, and saw the light from Morgan's invite him in. Quiet, but alive. Nothing else open on Manchester but a White Castle, which is a little bit too much action for him.

Castor's thirty five, a loner. Likes driving the truck. He goes down to Arkansas a couple days a week and spends a lot of time driving local in St. Louis. He'll go where he has to go, but Kansas, Nebraska, Wyoming, it threw him off. He can drive to Little Rock, Texarkana, even Dallas and back without paying attention to much of anything. He knows all the roads, the truck stops, and the stupid things people do along the way. Kansas drivers were stupid in different ways from those in northern Arkansas. Plus, it's too long away from Mom.

Maplewood is right west of St. Louis. Castor lives a couple blocks from the county line, so it all seems the same to him.

Not so for Tim Dawson. He puts the I.Q. of Maplewood at about eighty-six. Tim lives a few blocks up from Castor, but he's never seen the man before he steps into Morgan's. Tim likes Morgan's because of all the trucker types that go there. Especially for breakfast. Truckers, construction workers, and mustached guys eating eggs and pancakes, ignoring Tim's covert gaze. Morgan's changed so many times. First it was B&L, then it was Choy's Diner, and suddenly it turned into Morgan's 24 Hour. Then they zapped the 24 hour so they could close on Sundays.

Tim likes looking at guys in here. Never met any friends, but there is always a chance. Castor looks like a chance. Dressed in denim, with curly dark blond shaggy hair, a trim beard, and an oversize mustache. Not bad looking, not good looking, lost a little in what could be thought. Tim leaves an empty stool between them and orders a salad and a fries. He doesn't want to eat much, but Castor brooks a bit of hunger inside him. Just a nameless man. A male essence, an aura hanging over a cigarette and a dirty plate. Tim wonders what he might have to say. About anything.

But not that I think he's good looking, at least compared to everyone here, Tim thinks. Tim's twenty three and lives alone, a smooth, light-

2

skinned, delicate guy with brownish-blond hair and a mustache, and cute as can be. It's the mustache that does so much for him, a big wasp of fluff on his upper lip. It took him two years to grow it.

He's a little too bright-eyed and exuberant for this place, this time of night. He's almost embarrassed about it. Just shrugs it off and waits. Castor takes a glance at Tim, he tries to look disinterested, but finds his eyes roving over his body like maybe someday his hands would, or maybe his tongue...shit, why even get involved? Not with a stranger at Morgan's. The kid doesn't belong.

Too late for nonchalance. Tim catches the eyescan, he's forever on the lookout for that mixture of looks and sexuality that, blended with an hour in bed, turns instantaneously into lifelong true love. *Yeah, why not? No one's gonna hurt me here.* Besides that, Tim's got a Lesbian & Gay Pride 1986 T-Shirt on. Just kind of forgot about it for a second and wore it into the straight world. Most people didn't care anyway.

"How's it goin'?" Tim asks.

Castor rubs his hand down his face and nods. He's got those veins in the back of his hand that ramp up his masculinity. "Hey," he says. Or "hi." Or something like that. *Typical Maplewood shit,* Tim thinks. *Well, never mind... But I saw you looking!*

Castor smells something on the horizon and doesn't want to let go just yet. "Just got back...from...Kansas..." he spells out.

"Visiting?"

"Mm." Shake of the head, another fry in the mouth. "Drivin'. I'm a trucker."

Well that seals it for Tim. Big time. "Yeah?"

"Yep. All eighteen wheels. Usually go to Little Rock. Mid-south. They just shucked me over to Nebraska and then to Dodge City. Ain't nothin' goin' on there."

"You must be tired."

"Nah. I do it all the time."

"My name's Tim."

"Castor."

Tim puts his hand into Castor's calloused fingers and feels a hard warmth surrounding him. *Concentrate on it. It might be all you get.* "Good to meet you."

"Yeah." No emotion yet. Maybe not ever. "Mom stuck me with it."

"What?" Tim's confused.

"Castor. It's something mythological, I think. I don't know what she was thinkin'. She ain't usually all that mythological."

"I'm surprised you ain't heard of me," Tim says. "Dawson. Remember the Dawson family?"

"Nope."

"We were all over the papers a couple years ago."

"I don't read the papers. And I'm not here all that much."

"Family got killed. Drunk driver hit my mom, my dad, my brother, and my sister. Big time news."

"Sorry."

"Yeah." Tim hurt bringing it up, but someone always did. Just figured to get it out of the way as soon as he could.

"My sister might as well be dead," Castor says. He's more comfortable but looking straight ahead.

"What's wrong?"

"Got an education." Makes him angry. "Sonia Williams. Rutledge, now. Got an education, married, and moved out. She don't like me no more. She's too smart."

"We all got along pretty well. Be glad you got a family to fight with."

"Yeah, I know. She married a good man, anyway. Treats him like

4

shit, but he stays there."

Almost a dead giveaway, Tim thinks. *'Married a good man,' my foot.*

Castor brings out a billfold with a couple pictures. Sonia, a lithe, long-haired blonde, and Ricky Rutledge, her husband. Tim does a double take. He's never seen such a good-looking man.

Looks up at Castor with an unspoken smile. Finally the ice opens. Castor smiles back. "Yeah. I know what you mean."

Tim's eyes brighten for Castor as he gets his salad and fries.

"What you doin' out here so late, anyway?" Castor asks. "On a Thursday."

"Just kinda high," Tim said. "Wrote a song. I'm a musician, and I've been working on something, and it's *finished,* " he says triumphantly. "Took forever."

"What kind of stuff you do?" Castor asks.

"Dance music, mostly. Like they play in bars."

"I don't go."

"Never seen you. I've been trying to get Magnolia's or someone to play my stuff. I think they'll do this one. I don't have much. No records or anything, but I've been on the radio here."

"Sounds good."

"I'll let you hear it sometime."

"Sure."

Castor looks about thirty-five to him, but he's had it tough. Face a little weathered, eyes a little distant, hair a little thin in front, but kind of hairy everywhere else. Maybe. Just a guess. A hope. "Just felt like walking for a bit. Thought I'd take my song up to the bar tomorrow. Kinda have this dream of them putting it on and everybody running out to the floor to dance to it. It's a start, anyway."

"Too loud for me," Castor says slowly. "I don't like the people there

5

much. Me and Ricky go out every now and then. When she lets him, we go drinkin' out at the Landing. Down by the river." Old warehouse district downtown. Loud, lots of beer, lots of trouble for guys who don't fit in.

"Well, I don't like that," Tim says, "so we're even." A little silence, a few smiles, a few crunches on the salad. Tim wants to reach out to touch Castor's arm, feel for the dark masculinity under the jean jacket. But this is Morgan's, not Magnolia's. Tim puts a hand on the stool next to him like an invitation.

"Yeah I know," Castor says for no apparent reason.

"You're reading my mind."

"Nothin' else in here to read."

A few people come and go. They talk quiet. Personal conversation sounds odd here for some reason. Some guy at the other end is having a loud one with the server. About what his wife will and won't do. Somehow it doesn't seem personal at that volume. It's public. Everyone knows about her because they've heard that same conversation for fourteen years, but nobody ever sees her.

Tim eats a few French fries, playing around with them a little. *You know what this could be*, he says with no words.

"I'm about ready to head on, I think," Castor says. "Been good to meet you."

Tim's heart is sinking into the stool.

Castor summons up a little courage. It's not easy for him, but it's not all that hard. If you say it like it doesn't matter, it's not hard at all. "You comin'? I live over on Bleeck Avenue."

"Sounds promising," Tim says, but Castor doesn't pick up.

"Mom's there, but she's sleepin'."

"I live alone."

6

"Yeah. I just want to get home. It's okay. She's cool. She's just kinda sick, and I figured I might as well stay and take care of her when I'm here. But she knows about me. No big deal. Anyway, her room's in the front and mine's in the back. You're welcome to come by if you want. Just kick back."

"Yeah, Castor, I'd like to. I think it'd be cool." Castor looks like a lost soul to him at this moment. Like there was color in his eyes, in his face, but it got lost in the back of a truck. Maybe he can bring Castor back to life for a little. Trucker, thirties, super beard, super mustache, good body, rugged, warm. A man in any event. Maybe a six or seven on the ten scale but inviting enough, more man than he's had near him in his lonely life for sure.

Castor doesn't do this too much. Maybe here or there at the truck stop, maybe a straight guy here and there. He kind of feels straight anyway. Just likes sleepin' with guys is all. They walk out to go home on a cool April morning. Quickly, because it's a little breezier than it was before. And a little in a hurry.

Manchester's pretty deserted now. No buses, a few lights, a few left-over daffodils. Tim has all he needs. Can't wait to curl up with this guy, a fitting end to finishing his dance song. A little triumph to follow the artistic with the social, then follow the social with the sexual.

"Castor was Helen of Troy's brother," Tim says on the way home.

"Was he?"

"Castor and Pollux. They were twins. One was mortal and one was immortal, so they traded places every day so they could live forever."

"Which one was I?"

"I don't know," Tim says. "Which would you rather be?"

"Driving a truck for the next twenty million years, yeah," Castor muses. "Might finally get somewhere. Yeah, I can see it. Oh, my mama musta had a brain at some time or other. She reads a lot. That's all she's got to do."

"What's wrong with her?"

"Just shit. A little diabetes, a little this, a little that. She can't get around. Sonia pissed her off. Sonia's too good for her." Castor's getting hotter and hotter, seeing this cute young guy interested in him, turned on to him. It's not the type that usually likes him. But he almost feels like popping a beer and turning on the late movie instead. Chuck it now, before it gets out of hand. *No, this oughta work. He's a kid, he'll do what I want.*

Manchester to Ecoff, south a little to Bleeck Avenue. Tim walks a little behind, following Castor to the ends of the earth. It seems close enough, anyway, this little backwater side street, small house with a dim light in the darkness, the '58 Ford parked in the driveway, green and white with fins.

"My dad bought it new," Castor says. "I keep it runnin.'"

"Looks good," Tim says. Cars aren't his thing.

"You look mighty good yourself," Castor replies.

"Yeah? Thank you."

"You think I'm okay, right? You kinda turned on?"

"You know it."

"Thought so. I like it." Castor doesn't get romantic. That's about it.

Key in the door, opens up to a fifties museum. The rug, the furniture, the pictures on the wall, the lamp shades. The things that passed for taste thirty five years ago have never been updated here. Tim wonders what to say, but figures he'd better keep quiet. He doesn't know much about this mysterious trucker. Through the living room, down the hallway. One side a closed door, hiding the sick Emma Williams in her lair. On the other side, the door to paradise.

8

Castor stops off in the kitchen to get his beer, takes Tim into the bedroom, closes the door and flips on the TV. "Just a reflex," he says. "I'm not really even awake." He sits on the bed up against the wall. "Come on, guy," he says. "I don't know much about this romantic shit, you know."

"Maybe I'll show you," Tim says. He looks around at the dull green walls, a couple photos, old furniture. He's been dying for a touch of Castor's tough hand ever since they started walking home. Since before that. He takes it, feels it, puts it in his mouth. Castor doesn't say much. "I like Castor."

"Huh?"

"The name. It's a hot name. And you're a hot guy."

"You think so?"

"Yeah," Tim whispers with a smile. "Big time yeah."

Castor turns to look into Tim's eyes. A long stare, a bit of a smile, trying to figure out what to do.

Tim doesn't know if he's supposed to make a move or just sit there and watch TV. Castor doesn't know if he can stay awake enough to care. But it feels good to have someone there. It doesn't happen often. Not in his little castle. Just every now and then, some guy for a night, or when Ricky's too drunk to drive home. Castor always makes sure Ricky's too drunk to drive home.

Tim slowly moves closer, eyes on the prize, looks at the mustache, wants to feel it, closer, closer, touching his, brushing into it, finally lips touching together, feel it, feel it, make it work...

Castor moans into Tim's mouth and feels his hands under his jacket, pulling it off, feeling his arms for hair, muscle, feels Tim's tongue probe under his lip, pushing him down, almost helpless, but he wants to be, letting this guy who's so turned on to him use him so delicately.

Finally, Tim lets him up to pull off his t-shirt. Castor sighs deeply and smiles. "You know it's all bull about truckers having those bodies," he says. "You just sit there all day long and listen to '70s rock. Don't build any muscle."

"I'm sure it's fine." Tim trails his hands up Castor's body as he takes off the shirt. Gazes over a hairy chest. *I could live with this. I could.* "I could very easily..." he says aloud without thinking... "deal with this."

"Go for it." Castor is still distant, but there's a man in the room, doing what Castor wants done but is scared to ask for. He allows himself the luxury of looking Tim over, all over, staring at his face with no shame, watching Tim's hands play over his body, wanting finally to return the feeling, return the kiss, return the loss of control he feels. *Kid's probably done this a thousand goddamn times* floats through his head, but so what? "You wore that shirt into Morgan's?"

"Yeah. I forgot I had it on. I just wear them all the time."

"You're really into this gay thing."

"It's what I am. I like it. No reason to hide it."

"Well, I can't have you wearin' that here," Castor chuckles. He clutches at Tim's clothes and pulls them off with strong truckdrivin' hands. *Take your time, I don't want to miss anything.* Castor jumps up to turn off a light, and shadows from the TV set dance over the room, an odd assortment of lights and colors hitting the window from an old model Zenith.

Tim crawls next to Castor's warm body, lets it engulf his mind, just to feel it, closer, closer.

"With 'Great Songs of the Sixties,' we can relive those years, and now you can, too!" says some amphetamine-happy woman on the TV set. Snippets of forty different songs roll into Tim's brain and quickly fade under Castor's touch.

10

Thoughts race through his mind as he lets out some long breaths—*trucker, truck stop, trucker guys...AIDS!*

"What is it?" Castor asks.

"Nothing," Tim says. He files it back somewhere in his mind. Pretends it can't happen here. Throws Castor on his back, lays him out, puts his arms over his head, smells sweat that originated in Dodge City, lets himself go, drool, drip, drip all over the man.

Castor's overwhelmed by a feeling of giving up. *Somebody will really do this to me, damn Timmee, I never knew...*

Finally nothing but a little breathing, one man to another, scraping across hair, flesh, Castor gasps, grits his teeth, Tim watches. It's his man. *Yeah, come on, Castor, come on trucker, you can do it...yeah.*

Tim feels engulfed in Castor's hard hands, falling, falling, *I am yours, at your feet...I am all...GOD!! All yours.*

Castor's drooped on his back on the bed, and Tim falls over him, taking advantage of a newfound familiarity in a relationship maybe two hours old. Maybe it will last forever, maybe he won't die from this. He feels so good next to Castor.

Castor can't come up with words. "Yeah," is all he can think of. The rest sticks to him.

"Yeah?" Tim asks. "Yeah, I guess so. You are a hot truckin' man."

Also a tired truckin' man. He falls asleep for a while, and Tim sits up next to Castor's dripping body and clings to him. He's so buzzed from the song he wrote and picking someone up out of Morgan's Diner, he can't get to sleep. *This looks good,* he thinks. Maybe he did good enough that he can come back. You never know. You can pour your heart out to a guy and next thing you know, you're used garbage.

The woman from the sixties is back on TV.

"Now we can relive those years, and you can, too!"

Tim was born in 1968, so reliving is not an option for him. Who cares? She's part of his life now. And Castor's lying there. Tim looks him over. Every now and then, someone comes along he can just hold. He grasps Castor, lays his head on his shoulder, and closes his eyes.

That damn phone call rings in his mind sometimes, back when he was twenty or so, the call that says, *you're all alone, Dawson. Whole family's dead.* Well, the guy's in jail now. What a help.

* *
*

Somewhere around ten o'clock, Castor opens his eyes and looks calmly around the room with no reaction to seeing Tim gazing at him like he's wearing a halo.

"Hi Timmee," Castor says. "Still here, I see."

"Got nowhere to go."

"I got to work today. In the afternoon. Drive around the city a little."

Tim kisses Castor good morning. Not that he slept anyway. "Not me."

"You don't have to work today?"

"I don't work."

"Then how do you live?"

"Insurance and inheritance. I got everyone's life insurance policies. My dad had a bundle. I rent our old house out. Too hard to live there after all that. I bought a buncha musical equipment—I always wanted it, and all this money kinda showed up. I live off interest and rent. Got a little apartment on Waldemar. Just a few blocks away from here."

"Why don't you live in the house?"

"Can't afford it. Like, in my heart, can't afford it. And interest from my savings gets lower and lower each year. I'm doin' okay. I'd rather work on songs than make a lot of money. Maybe someday I can do both." Tim traces a finger along Castor's chest, then on down. "Looks like interest is going up."

Castor smiles. "You just can't get enough, can you?"

"Lucky for you, Castor." Tim likes saying the name. He's never called a guy Castor before. "Well, hey, you wanna come with me to Magnolia's tonight? Hear the song?"

"I'll be drivin' till around ten or so."

"You can come then."

"Nah. I don't like goin' out."

"Well what do you do?"

"Stay here. Beer, TV, mom. I can't get into all those gay guys."

"So, you don't really meet people."

"People aren't my thing."

"So you don't, like, go dancing or anything." Gay men staying in? Who'd have thought?

Castor looks like he's coming out of another planet. "Nooo. I don't dance. I just—you already seen all what I do. Hey, you know you can come by later after that. If you want. Just to hang out. I'm not lookin' for any big emotional thing, but if you wanna come by every now and then and mess around, watch TV, yeah, sounds good."

"Yeah. I'll be by. I don't know about tonight, but…" *Fuck Tim, yes you do!* a voice calls to him from the subconscious. "I'll see what I can do. Sometimes I close down the bar. If the song goes over well, I'll see what comes out of it."

Castor takes a trip to the bathroom, comes back and flops on top of Tim. All the slime of last night clings to him like a velvet dawn. He reeks of sweat and cum, that breath that seems like a troop of soldiers camped out in his mouth, but hell, it's for real. It all builds up again.

13

You meet, and it seems like it can go on forever. Castor can't remember the last time he's been laid twice in a day. Or if he ever cared enough about it.

"Damn, you are good, Timmee. You been around a lot?"

"No, just smart. Make it up as I go. And I like makin' you feel good. I think you could use it. Looks like you just need to let go a little, that's all."

"I'm pretty happy the way I am."

"Well," Tim says, with nothing to base it on, "I'm pretty happy the way you are, too."

CHAPTER 2

"You think you're bitter enough, Tim?"

Tim looks up at Chuck the DJ with an admiration usually reserved for saints. "Try living my life, Chuck."

"It's really good. I think it'll take off. I think I can work it in about midnight or so."

Tim already made arrangements with Chuck to meet him early and give the song a preview. Chuck's been good to him, but he's never played anything. And to be honest, Tim's never done anything this good from a production point of view. It was never a question that he couldn't write, but whether he could create something that sounded original yet at the same time sounded like everything else. To stand, so to speak, as a man among men in the world of loud dance music.

But it's only seven o'clock, and Tim's got five hours to wait. He really likes Chuck. To a point, anyway. Chuck's a dark-haired slightly overweight guy with a thick stubble all over his face. Always. Big black mustache, thick hairy arms. Bright blue eyes. And he spins music, so all the rest is gravy. Tonight, he makes Tim's dream come true. The song. A month or so of work on this one. All his songs seem to be based on Magnolia's experiences. Tim wonders sometimes if he could exist without Magnolia's. Or if Mag's could exist without him. It's his other home.

He has a good time there. With his cuteness, his mustache, his personality, and his crystal clear complexion, he averages three propositions a night. Just happens that way. Once he even went home with two guys, the first at nine and the second at two. Didn't plan on it, but the first one kicked him out immediately after orgasm, and the second seemed a little friendlier. But it doesn't happen that way often.

He tries to hide the real story. The gnawing loneliness. The feeling of being all by himself in a south Dogtown apartment. No, the bar won't close down if he stops going. Maybe a few people would ask after him, but life would go on. Sex is a panacea, like alcohol for some, and these days just as dangerous.

Maybe Castor will care about him. It's killing him to know Castor's home watching TV, and he could be there with him. If only the song didn't go on *tonight*! Everything happens at once. Or nothing happens at all.

He's got to tell someone about it. About Castor. About picking up a guy out of Morgan's Diner in Maplewood. He's so proud of himself, so happy to find a man who asked him to come back. And meant it. They all say they want to see you again, and you call, and they're real nice, but there's never time. Castor has time, at least. *Maybe I can skedaddle at 12:06! No, I need to be here. It's Friday night. My Friday night. I need to see the effects of the song. If anyone listened to it.*

About eleven thirty he goes up to the DJ booth to wait it out. Chuck puts his arm around Tim for a little while. "Get control of yourself, man."

"Here?" His mind wanders back to Castor. He could have been there for a few hours. *Hopefully he hasn't forgotten me.* Well, maybe for a few minutes it will all go away. For a few minutes, he can just hear his music blasting over the speakers. At Magnolia's, even. And for a few minutes, the dream will be there, then on to the other bars, a label contract? Take it one day at a time. Any little victory will do over the dregs of lifelessness.

It's just after Jody Watley, who's just after Madonna. First a throw-back to "Holiday," then Jody comes on with a medley. "Still a Thrill," "Looking for a New Love," "Don't You Want Me," and then Tim Daw-son starts: tambourine (electric, of course), the bass drum beats, the snare on the after-beats—nobody's left the floor yet. Finally we get go-ing. The high staccato over droning synth chords, loud as can be, but never loud enough for Tim. Some guy shrieks with delight, and the music goes right through his brain. Tim's voice comes wipsy out over the speakers, in stereo, with backups, verse, chorus—the whole thing swirls in his head. He can't believe it.

They're out there, dancing, gyrating, sniffing poppers, pounding the wood floor in rhythm to Tim's drumbeats. He's done it. He's cre-ated the atmosphere, highlighted the evening:

How come I can touch you but you won't let me love you
How come I can kiss you but you won't let me stay
Why you say you want me if you won't let me have you
Why's it wrong tomorrow if it seems so right today

Okay, it isn't great art, but it makes its point. At 120 decibels on the dance floor, it takes on a meaning all its own for those men and women smart enough to read between the lines. It's happened to them so many times they've forgotten it's not acceptable.

Tim's smiling, has a hand on Chuck's leg just for validation. Chuck is holding Tim's hand because he probably hopes to be paid back for this later. The second chorus goes by—a great build up! Now back to the loneliness of drums and droning synth chords. The high staccato, the repeat chorus, fade out... He sees his friend Dale Terrell on the dance floor wave to him. *You finally got it done, hey Timmee?* Chuck plays the whole thing, all five minutes and forty seven seconds of it, and makes a little announcement at the end that Tim's the one that did it.

His triumph is complete.

An old copy of "Shake Your Body" replaces it and suddenly it's wiped off the face of the earth for a short while, but Tim's on air. He knows Chuck will play it again. He knows they loved it. It worked, and he can feel like a real person for just a little while now.

The smile won't go away. Dale comes up to him and hugs him.

"Fabuloso, Tim!" Dale hangs out on the east side of the dance floor. Most of the Black guys do, but the unwritten racial dividing line gets fainter and fainter over time. It's a a voluntary segregation people notice from time to time. If they cared enough, they'd move over.

"Thanks!"

"Great song," say a few guys leaving the dance floor. You can't say much else when it's so damn loud.

Dale lives right below Tim in a four-family on Waldemar. He's heard the bass drum more times than he cares to mention. "I never heard that one before."

"I wanted to surprise you."

"You're gettin' better and better. You're gonna go somewhere."

Maybe some hi-tech music executive is somewhere in the bar. Maybe. Someone pulls Tim over in the next room.

"Have you been doing this for awhile? Have you heard of The Cure, The Church, The Bronski Beat? Do you have any more songs?"

"Yeah, I've got lots."

"I'd like to hear them."

"Maybe you can come by sometime."

"What you doin' right now? God, you're real hot! And talented, too." His admirer runs his fingers through the mustache. "This is nice."

He must be about forty five or so, graying hair, good shape, friendly, but with the eyes of a one night stand. Tim's got better than that now.

"Thanks. Maybe some other time. You're hot, yourself." *Not that it matters if you are, I'll say it anyway.* Tim gives the guy a kiss and feels a tongue trying to part his lips but he won't let it in. He's got better than that. Finally.

Tim's got on a pair of jeans and a torn 1984 St. Louis Lesbian and Gay Pride t-shirt. It's got a few holes here and there but some guy always sticks his fingers in them, so wearing it makes it worthwhile for him. He'd always get some kind of affection at Mag's. It was hard to hold out, but he knew if he went home with everyone, he'd be real sick real fast. Yeah, affection generates into sex here and there, but rarely with a chance for a repeat offense.

He's glad he's got his looks. The bright brown eyes, the straight nose some people say sticks out too far, hair he doesn't mess with much. Just wash, dry, and he's got a whole day ahead of himself with nothing to do. Maybe one day he'll start working out, add a little meat. Maybe. But his appearance gives him a chance to escape. In the gay world, looks are enough of an asset. Sometimes he falls into the same trap himself.

All night spent hoping someone will tell him they loved the song. People do. Talking to Dale, crossing the invisible race demarcation line, dancing, already thinking of the next song so it can happen again. He waits for the unaccompanied percussion in the beginnings and breaks of the other songs and sings his own melodies over them. If only he could have brought his trucker up to show to everyone. *Look, guys, I have someone! Someone you've never seen.* Not just another bar slut on the revolving door of the sex/romance merry-go-round, but a real man.

19

Tim's hardly slept since Thursday, so he spends most of Saturday in bed, wobbling around the apartment trying to get some energy and occasionally blasting his song through headphones, marveling at his genius. *Yeah, this 16 track studio has opened the whole world for me.*

Thanks, Dad.

Round about seven o'clock, Tim wakes up from his third nap of the day, takes a shower, and goes through the motions: blow dry, brush, shave, throw on some clothes that don't smell, and off he goes to the Williams' stronghold.

Castor's in the living room on a couch; his mother Emma Williams is sitting on a chair with a ball of yarn, a book, a cat, a pack of cigarettes, and a remote control.

Tim doesn't know what to do with the situation, and he's real uncomfortable in the dark house that smells like smoke. Emma's kind of portly, grey hair in a bun, and it looks to Tim like she'd have a really hard time just getting out of the chair—as if it only happened once or twice a week. She's not pretty, but maybe there's a little resemblance between her and her son if you look hard. It gets into Tim's mind how this woman could name a baby Castor. You'd think Mike or Fred, but not an unusual stud name like Castor.

"This's Mom, this's Tim," Castor says. "Have a seat."

Tim sits on the other end of the couch. *Can't she leave? Can't we go to your room?* He wants so bad to touch his man again and doesn't know how to go about it. He's never had a date where the guy's mother was in the room.

They watch for awhile and nobody says too much.

"How'd it go last night?"

Finally. "Good, real good. I brought a tape of it by so you could hear it."

"Okay," Castor says. Does not care. Dance music isn't his thing.

"They really danced to it. Liked it."

"Proud o' yourself, ain't ya?"

"Mm hmm."

"Good."

This is awful.

"Go on, sit next to him already," Emma breaks in authoritatively. "I know he didn't invite you over here to watch *The Golden Girls.*"

Castor puts his white t-shirted arm out on the couch and beckons with his eyes. Tim's over like a metal to a magnet. Gets his shoulder up in Castor's armpit. "Better?"

"Yep." Now it doesn't matter what they do. He could watch *Gilligan's Island* re-runs all night for all he cared, long as he could be close to Castor.

Castor hasn't had a shower all day. It's his day off, and he doesn't care what goes on, really. No shower. Just hang out at home, sleep, TV, beer, mow the lawn, hasn't really thought a helluva lot about Tim, but yeah, it has crossed his mind. Lying in bed, thinking what Tim did, trying to recreate it as best as he could. He would need Tim for that.

"Sonia called when you were out," Emma says.

"Yeah. What's she want?"

"Ricky's mom's having a party. Dave's turning sixteen."

Dave is Sonia's nephew, Ricky's brother's kid. Ricky doesn't have any kids. He's been married about three years now. "She's gotta let me fuck her first," Ricky used to say, so people stopped asking.

"Whole family's gonna be there, and Sonia says we might as well come along. Says Ricky asked for you."

"Let's go! You oughta see this Rutledge mama, she's a scream," he says to Tim.

"I can go," Tim says cautiously.

Castor looks at Mom.

"Bring 'im. No reason you can't bring a date. Betty's gonna shit, but that's about what she's good for."

"That's Ricky's mom. She's kinda proper. She shits about a lotta stuff she don't need to."

"See," Emma says to Tim to clarify. "Sonia thinks 'cause she went to college and she married money that she's too good for us white trash folks. She forgets who put her through school."

"She hardly comes back here," Castor says.

"She's a smart girl, too. She got a three-seven average in college. Got a scholarship the last year. Got a job as an accountant. Then she married that Ricky Rutledge."

Castor puts up the defense. "Don't you start goin' on Ricky."

"Castor's the only one in the family what can stand the man," Emma puts in. "Even Sonia knows she made a mistake."

"He'd be fine if she was decent to him. You should hear what he tells me."

"Yeah. He's always flappin' off at the mouth around you. He's always drunk around you, too."

"I'm sure Tim don't need to hear any more about it, Mom."

"I'm sure he'll find out soon enough."

Castor turns to look Tim in the eye. "Lookin' forward to it now, I bet."

"Every minute."

"Ricky's a good guy," Castor says.

"You're a good guy," Tim says real quiet like, and Castor grips his shoulder a little tighter. Tim's tape is burning in his pocket. He wants so bad for Castor to hear it, to get into it, to *approve* of it, but he doesn't think it's going to happen. Castor doesn't look like the type. *Well, accept it. You're sitting here close to the guy you want to be close to, it's okay. No it's not, but deal with it.*

Tim doesn't know what to make of all this. Looks around the room. Some of those ten dollar oil paintings on the wall, but they were only three dollars when Mr. Williams bought them on a street corner. He gets a whiff of Mrs. Haversham from *Great Expectations*. The whole house just kind of stopped in 1955.

"Your dad live here?"

"Don't *mention* his name!" Emma says almost comically.

"He just kind of disappeared about ten or twelve years ago," Castor tells Tim. "We ain't seen him since. I don't really give a shit."

"Castor tells me your family got wrecked in a drunk driving accident."

"Yep." *Here we go again.*

"Sorry to hear that."

"Mom, we'll see you later."

"Pleasure to meet you, Tim."

"Same here."

Castor gets Tim off the couch and walks him into the bedroom— the castle—his arm still around his new friend. Tim likes being taken away like this. And out of that dungeon of a living room. It's too odd in there. No, he can't see Sonia staying in that house. He hasn't even met her yet, but just her picture and the Bleeck House, as Tim begins to think of it, they don't go together. Where she would even sleep, he had no idea.

Castor lights up a cigarette. "Less than a pack a day."

"I never smoked."

"You're smart. Things ain't bad, though. They'll kill ya', but I don't see any point in prolonging *this*."

"Wanna hear my song?"

"Guess I have to if I wanna get any, right?"

"Right." Tim puts it in the stereo, if you can call it a stereo. In fact, it's from the days when it was called a stereo because it made a difference. He turns out the overhead light, putting on an old lamp by the bed instead. He can see a little of Magnolia's, relive it, see Dale wave at him from the dance floor, see the guys saying "great song," looks in Castor's eyes to try to see any reaction. *The words, can you hear them? Does it ring a bell, or you're not into this?* Maybe Castor isn't into it. Avoids the pain by staying away from it all. And misses all the highs because of it. Not worth it. *I may be emotional, but give me my gay scene.*

Castor's laying on the bed. Tim's already got Castor's shirt off, playing with his chest during the song. Just make sure he's paying attention. *That's my soul in the stereo.*

"Not bad!" Castor's impressed as he can be. For dance music. "That you singin'?"

"Yeah," Tim whispers.

"Yeah. Interesting voice."

"Thanks." Tim looks deep into Castor's eyes. He looks perfect. Just the way a man should look. Everything else is a variant. This is all a man needs to look right. "Oh, I want you, Castor."

"Well take it." Just a little too Barbara Cartland for him to process. And Castor knows because his mother owns the whole redundant romantic collection of hers.

"You really like my song?"

"Yeah, I really do."

"Cause it's okay if you don't."

"Don't worry about what everyone thinks, Timmee. Particularly me. I don't know that much."

Castor looks at Tim. *Why is it so damn hard? Just do it.* Pulls Tim to him for a kiss. Pries open Tim's mouth and sticks his tongue way down. Just to lose himself for awhile.

Yeah, the hours of TV were worth this, Tim thinks. Not being at Magnolia's. They'd all rather be here, to feel it, feel lost in the man you want. *It's what we live for. Why go out?*

It's a triumph tonight to see Castor's face turned back to the wall, biting his lip, all the hair on his head and his face a sweaty sculpture over his features. He gasps out "Oh" a little louder than intended, finally globs cum all over Tim's hand. Tim looks down at this goopy mess on his fingers, smiles. God, what he wouldn't give to swallow it, slurp it down, drip it down his face. Could be poison. What can you do? He never has tasted it. He was born too late.

Tim looks over Castor's sweaty, hairy body like it's something he created. Like a song, maybe. Whatever it was, Castor wouldn't be in that place if not for Tim. Not like that. It was awful good.

Castor lets out a deep breath. "Man, you work me like an oil derrick, you know?"

"Gusher," Tim says.

"Yeah," Castor grunts out. "White gold?" He sits up on the bed. For a minute, he says nothing, just rubs his eyes, gets himself together, and finally throws Tim down. "You must think we're one crazy family." Castor transports Tim to Never Never Land, maybe Cloudcuckooland ...visions of Magnolia's...the pink neon *Mags!* sign on the window flashes through his eyes, the song intro plays over and over, those high staccato notes that become Castor's fingers, his mustache scorching Tim's body. Castor gets closer, farther away, closer, wet surprises in between drumbeats. He looks up at Castor's face. *It's for real. It's for real, and nothing else ever matters.*

CHAPTER 3

"Did this car myself, mostly," Castor says. "Redid the engine twice, painted it, fixed the fenders, put the seat belts in the back. Never used to care if your kids went through the windshield," he laughs. Maybe Dad didn't.

"Looks good," Tim says. Cars aren't his thing.

"Looks damn good."

"Rides good from back here."

"Thanks." That puts Castor in a good mood.

Tim's in the back, and Castor and his mom are in the front. They're on their way to Ted and Betty Rutledge's house. *Home*, rather. Betty's a big family person, and she has them all together about once a month to celebrate one event or other. Keep in contact, she figures, because in the long run, family's all you have that you can count on. She's drilled it into them for years now, and most of them believe it. Whether they like each other or not, they stick together.

They're driving down Highway 40, out west past Clarkson Road where there are lots of big homes and rich people. For Tim, it's the end of the universe. He doesn't know anybody out there. Outside of Mag's and Dogtown, he doesn't know a heck of a lot. It's a good half hour drive from Bleeck Avenue.

Everyone's dressed reasonably nice, depending on the definition of reasonably. Emma isn't going to get too dolled up. First of all, she

27

doesn't have anything, and second of all, it's too uncomfortable. Some-times just walking is too uncomfortable. She can't even remember how she got that way, just that she *is* that way. Tim's got on pleated pants and a dress shirt, Castor has on the "Goddamn Rutledge Outfit." So-nia bought it for him because he was always looking like too much of a trucker at these parties. "And you know you wouldn't be there if it wasn't for Ricky."

"Yeah. I'm the only one who talks to him anyway." So, he wears navy blue pants and a light pink shirt. You can kind of see through it because it's light. Sonia didn't notice that when he tried it on and has rued the day ever since. It doesn't matter, because he still looks like a trucker. And he acts like a trucker. Just to aggravate her. "It's what I am," he said to her once. Why bother? It's all in how you say it. *A trucker.*

Castor and Ricky became best friends real soon after they met, af-ter Sonia brought him home and said, "Mom, this is Ricky and we're going to be married." None of the relatives could really understand or approve of this friendship between the two social misfits. The Rutledg-es vaguely acquiesced to Castor's bizarre homosexuality. Sonia made it an issue, and while Ricky's parents assured her they had no issue with Castor's sexuality, they weren't thrilled about Ricky hanging out with a rather dubious character, gay or not.

Emma thought Ricky was a shit to Sonia from the beginning, not to mention thoroughly obnoxious in his own right.

"What does Castor know about anything?" Sonia would say to Ricky. "He doesn't know culture, he doesn't know classical music, he doesn't know anything. Why do you even like him?" She'd had enough of her brother growing up and was hoping to escape, not have her own husband fall for his antics.

"You don't know anything but what I taught you," Ricky said. "You were just as much trucker as he is. You know Mother wanted a damn morganatic marriage, so I'd shut up if I were you."

"Why do you listen to her?"

"I don't. I married your ass, didn't I?"

Castor and Ricky were friends, and that was that. They went out every now and then and had this bond between them that worried a lot of people because nobody could see any reason for it. Betty and Ted certainly didn't raise their son to associate with such people.

Tim's in awe of the house when they pull up in the driveway. Castor helps Emma out of the car, and she canes her way up the walk to the front door. Rows of tulips and faded daffodils all along the walkway. Rare tulips: purples, greens, odd stuff that costs an arm and a leg. And they're all standing up straight.

About five o'clock on Sunday now, and everyone's there already. Ricky's got a brother and a sister, both married, both with children. There are a few stray relatives here and there, whatever Mrs. Rutledge can find, and these damned in-law Williams, and "Who's that, Ted?"

"'This here's Timmee," Castor says with a manufactured pride. "He's my new... friend."

Tim hears lover between the lines, but then again sometimes he's not that smart.

"It's a pleasure," Betty says.

"Good to meet you, too." Tim's never been to a family gathering on a date. It legitimizes his whole gay experience. *It can work—it can!*

Tim sees Ricky from the corner of the living room and his mouth almost drops open. The family's over it, they're used to him.

"Castor, my man!"

"Heyyyy, Rickyyyy!!!" Castor makes a fist with a hard hitting thumb-up, radiant, more life in him than Tim's ever seen. Almost scary.

29

They hug each other, a tough macho hug that goes on a little longer than it should. They're used to that, too. Ricky's just trying to say he accepts homosexuals more than the rest of them. Castor just wants a piece of any man he can get.

But Castor's mystified them. He's defied the stereotypical gay guy every turn of the way, and they can at least respect him for that if they can't respect him as a person.

"Who's the broad?" Ricky says to Castor.

Castor smiles. "It's Tim. Tim Dawson. Met him at Morgan's Diner."

"Yeah, another morganatic marriage." Ricky loves that word. Means if the king or the prince marries a commoner, she doesn't get his stuff. "Well, Tim, I'm very happy to meet you." He shakes Tim's hand. Warm and strong. Ricky's got hands that could give a hard-on to a dead man. Tim's in these thin pants, and he's got to work hard to keep himself under control. The whole world can see how he feels.

Ricky's a young looking thirty three, jet black hair, short, with a few bangs. Mustache, shadow, dark eyes, good-looking straight nose, bright lips, light complexion. Mustache curls over his lip ever so delectably. He's about five-ten, maybe one ninety, all muscle. Tim can see muscles and veins in his forearms. *Damn, he's hairier than Castor!* Some on his chest must stick out an inch and a half. Pushed out through the open collar. Ricky knows he's got a conquest, but he doesn't really think about it. Men aren't his thing. Usually. Maybe they are. No, they're not. Well, sometimes. No, he's married. It never stops.

He calls Sonia over, asks if she knows Castor's new friend.

No, I don't believe I do.

Tim takes a look and forms an impression on his own. It's not as bad as all the advance publicity led him to believe. She seems bouncy. Bouncy blonde hair, kind of straight with a curl at the end, a real tasteful party dress, brown eyes, pretty and doesn't look anything like Castor. Must be more like her father. Younger than Castor, she's about twenty seven, he figures. She puts out a hand to shake, and Tim takes to her.

Castor's surprised. He figured anything he brought over would be a *non grata* in Sonia's eyes. Tim's innocent looking, though. Maybe they'll get along.

There's some member of the family playing a piano in a corner of the living room. "C.P.E. Bach," Ricky says, "Sonata Number Five." Ricky knows it all. He never forgets a piece once he hears it. Sonia can be proud of him, he knows what he knows.

Tim takes a trip to the dining room. There's a table set with matching china for twenty. He's never seen this much china in his life. And a table that long! Looks like Betty's trying to fit in twenty one because no one said Tim was coming. No one had heard of Tim.

Or so they thought. Dave's heard of Tim. "Tim Dawson? You write songs?"

"Yeah!" *This is heaven.*

"I've heard you on the Todd Sampler! You've got some great stuff!"

Dave's kind of a big-boned guy, dark with an angular face and a big jutting nose, but heck, he's only sixteen so stop thinking of him like that. "Thanks," says Tim. No one's ever *heard of him* before. It's the biggest day of his life. Again! He almost forgot he had some songs played on the Todd Sampler. Maybe not good enough for dancing, but good enough for late-night radio. "You stay up for it?"

"I'd kill for the Todd Sampler!" Dave says.

The Todd Sampler goes out on KDHX-FM on Friday at about four o'clock in the morning. Plays all kinds of out of the way out dance music. It wreaks havoc with Dave's sleeping schedule and probably Todd's as well.

"Glad you like it."

"Yeah, I taped some of it. I like your synth."

Tim wants to say his latest was a hit at Mag's, but he wonders. Not in the mood to explain it all now.

The seating debacle begins. Tim's thrown the whole damn thing off, but they're too polite to say anything. Only the Williams's would bring an uninvited guest to a sit down dinner. Mrs. Rutledge taught her family a few things about etiquette that must have been forsaken in that bleak dark horse bungalow south of Dogtown. Who needs etiquette when nobody likes you?

Castor sits next to Ricky, and Tim next to him. Sonia's on Ricky's other side. She knows she's no competition, and she knows Ricky does it on purpose. He forgot the shit out of cleaving unto his wife. She wonders why they even mentioned it at the wedding.

Ricky can tell Castor about his job, and he listens. They talk about cars. Ricky loves the Ford. It's fascinating. The car's as old as he is and it runs better.

"I seen you do some pretty good runnin'," Castor tells him.

And Dave? He's only sixteen, and that's just today. More or less an excuse for this whole party, but other than a good reason to lay out some china, not all that important. He wants a car for his birthday, but he'll have to do with less. Maybe a stereo. He can turn it up, but he can't kill himself with it. Talk gets around that Dave isn't doing as well as he should be. Maybe he doesn't deserve the stereo. Well, it's too late, he's got it now.

But Dave's fascinated with Tim, because Tim's a singer. *A singer, my God, I never thought of myself that way.*

Tim's fascinated with Ricky, and he's sure he'll see Ricky again because Castor likes him so much. Ricky's soooo good to look at. *Just close*

32

*the bedroom door with a photo of the man's face, and I've got the afternoon
taken care of,* Tim thinks.

After dinner, he gets to talking to Sonia because Castor's kind of
occupied. Besides that, he likes her. She's interesting, a bit hoosier and
a bit high culture at the same time. Got herself a rich husband and an
education. She's *made* something of herself, and it comes through in an
expository conversation. And she likes to dance. *Maybe we can go sometime. I'll show you Magnolia's.*

I'd like that.

"We on for next Saturday?"

"Damn sure we are!"

Ricky and Castor.

"I dread those two going out," Sonia tells Tim.

"What's the problem?" Tim sees a good chance to get some dope.
He barely knows Castor. His whole life set on this man, and it's been
four days. Things just change fast.

"Drink too much. I'm afraid one day one of 'em's gonna get themselves killed. You get Ricky into the beer and—"

Ricky overhears. "Aw, cut it out, honey."

Sonia laughs a little. "I'm not the one doing anything."

"I don't go out with him that much. I'm home with you all the time."

"Well," Tim says to her, "You can come out with me. Lots of girls
have a great time in a gay bar. And Ricky's got nothing to worry about."

"What about Castor?" Sonia asks.

"Castor ain't worried," Castor replies.

"Get worried," Tim says. He wants his man at least a little possessive.

Castor rubs Tim's head. Showing affection in polite society. Just
says, "Mm."

"Well, I think it sounds great," Sonia says.

Emma thinks it sounds ridiculous, as she puts it on the way home. "She never thought it sounded great before." This Tim guy's having an interesting effect on her children.

"She didn't like it because I did it," Castor said. Tim feels glad Sonia is in the family. She's a real person. And without her, Castor and Mom wouldn't have anything to talk about.

They're back home, and it's about ten o'clock in Castor's bedroom. Tim's got nothing to wear for the night, and he doesn't feel like leaving Castor for the ten minutes it might take him to go home and get something. Castor's got a dirty t-shirt, thrown on the floor from the last truck trip. That'll do. Put it on and feel him all around. It's too big, but he won't need it for long anyway. Castor's out of the Sonia Regiment uniform in no time at all, and he pops into bed with a beer. Lays on this back and flips on some stupid movie without sound.

Tim hops over to him, laying against him so an ant couldn't crawl between them. Yeah, the essence of the shirt and the real thing. The party was nice, but here's the real party. We know what's coming. Sometime soon.

"Ricky's pretty hot," he says. It's taboo to talk about one guy when you're on a date with another, but Tim can't help himself.

"You like him?" Castor asks. His arm keeps closing in on Tim when he takes a puff on the cigarette. He hasn't had one in six hours. Betty doesn't allow smoking in her house. She doesn't even allow it in her family.

"I've never seen anybody like that before. I mean, you're hot, but he's—"

"You're really into it, aren't you?"

"*You* like him," Tim said.

"I like him 'cause he's him."

"Yeah, right. Everybody at Mag's likes me because of who I am."

"Oh, man, Tim, don't start. It's been a hard day already. I'm not in the mood for nothin' heavy."

"Sorry." Real sorry. Didn't seem like such a big deal.

They lie together quietly for awhile, finally Tim gets out of Castor's shirt to be a little closer to him. He feels kind of full from the dinner and it's nice just to stay still without any fabric wrapped around his body. An interesting day. Still an outsider, but somehow a part of it all. A date with his boyfriend's sister. *Yeah, I guess that's getting in good, since he isn't gonna be available. Might as well do something.*

"I been with Ricky before," Castor says out of the blue. Maybe to brag.

"You mean you've slept with him?"

"Yeeeaaahhh. Couple times," he says, dreamy like.

"But he's your sister's husband."

"Uh huh. I know it. But she don't know it. She don't know I did it, so don't you go telling her."

"Is he gay?"

"Nope. Just me. He just...it just kinda happened. We never even talk about it. Just do it."

"You still do it now?"

Castor hesitates a little. "Nah." Tim picks it up but forgets it. He has to. *Well, you don't own the man in four days. Just want to.* "He don't do it 'less he's drunk, no-how. I don't think he gets enough at home. I don't think Sonia knows what to do. I always wondered about that."

His voice tone changes a little, more inward. "I always wondered about my sister layin' in bed. I can't imagine her and Ricky. Just can't."

* *
*

Or more like *don't want to,* but that's another story. Castor remembers every move he ever made with Ricky. Every touch, every word. It's the only time he ever felt like doing it because he liked the guy. The only time he could say, "I do this to show you how I feel." It was a bitch Ricky was married to begin with, worse yet it was his own sister, but those things come along like that on the turf of life. Whatever feeling he had for Ricky—that alien subculture idea of feeling at home with someone, feeling good around them, a feeling that hadn't hit him ever before then—he couldn't let go now.

Just about a year and a half ago, they went out and whooped it up all night. Castor needs it every now and then. Not too often, but here and there it gets to him, cooped up in the truck all day, at home all night, this and that truck stop in Arkansas or Texas or wherever.

Ricky needs it too. Cooped up in his office. Accounting. Always the damn accounting. Biggest mistake he made in his life, but he didn't have the aptitude to be a concert pianist. Never could learn the stuff.

So off they go to the Landing—Laclede's Landing, that part of downtown where West County yuppies and old warehouses combine to make party bars, specialty shops, and overpriced restaurants. Loud bands, booze, women, men all in pullovers acting like the women owe them something. Some of the women act like sluts but demand to be treated like ladies. Izods, Polos, high heels, bright red dresses; it's all a blur whizzing by over decorative cobblestone.

Castor doesn't mind all these straight people. He ain't lookin' anyhow. He's got Ricky, and that's entertaining enough. Ricky's family is so cultured. And sedate. They hate this going on. Man, he's over thirty, married, with an independent income, and he can't even go out with his fucking brother-in-law. Parents always on his back, so heavy he can't walk.

Shit on all that. Ricky drinks and drinks and drinks. Not often, but some nights his gullet gives way and he pours beer down him like water through a busted dam. One night—that first special night—Castor was drunk enough that he could make it home on auto-pilot, but not over to Ricky's place.

Ricky was too drunk to drive and knew it. Too dredged even to call the old lady. *Just stay here, you'll go home tomorrow.* Ricky passed out in Castor's bed. And Castor felt pretty good, his mind loose enough to think he was real happy going to sleep next to Ricky. Couldn't figure out why.

Sometime in the middle of the night, Castor felt this arm around his chest. Yeah. Ricky snuggled up to him like a cuddly bear or something. Felt good. Ricky had real strong arms. Strong body. He worked out. He wasn't even awake. Just a reflex. Ricky probably thought Castor was Sonia. Must have, anyway, because his dick was hard. Castor didn't even think about it, just kept feeling it against his leg.

He reached down and started messing with it. Didn't think about much. Didn't think about Sonia, just about himself. It seemed Ricky could use a little affection. The drunker he got, the lonelier he talked. A wife that doesn't care, a family that cast him out. Not physically; the Rutledges are too sophisticated for that. *If I was stupid, I wouldn't even know they did it.*

Castor listened to him moan for awhile under the stroke of his trucker-calloused hand and fingers. So easy to touch someone who doesn't know you're doing it. To feel for the unfeeling. Finally Ricky opened his eyes, his dream turned real. He looked at Castor with a quizzically disfigured smile. Confused. Finally figured it out. "You devil motherfucker," he said.

"Yeah."

"Stop that!"

"Okay." Hands up, Ricky like a beached whale.

"No, don't." It was better than nothing. And Ricky kind of liked guys, way back in his mind. If he thought about it hard enough. Family wouldn't let him, but yeah, he did.

"You make up your mind. You wanna cum, or you wanna just lay there thinkin' about it?"

"I can't think, I'm too drunk. You think for me."

Castor didn't figure getting anything back on this one. He knew the straight guy routine all too well. They just like to be done. No wonder their women didn't want to. Nothing in it for them. But this was different for Castor. Different feeling. He knew Ricky needed someone so desperately. "You know," Castor said, "I'm the only one that likes you out of the whole bunch."

"Yeah, I know now."

Castor remembered Ricky looking in his eyes the whole time. Remembered Ricky shot the big one and passed out. Remembered taking care of himself because Ricky was asleep. Not that it mattered. Nobody said anything the next day.

But then Ricky kept staying over when they'd go out. Every three weeks or so, is all. Not much contact in between, just a quick phone call or maybe a few hours at the family parties.

He's getting better at it, too, Castor thinks. Getting a little more responsive. Ricky will touch; he'll explore a bit. But it's such a damn

38

dream. Can't let Tim go over this. Tim seems like he'd go. Like he wants instant commitment, instant love, instant lifetime. Too much, too fast. Nobody's ever taken to him like this before. It's nice, but it's hard. How can love be there just because?

It's never been there at all.

CHAPTER 4

Ricky's had a weird upbringing compared to everyone else he knows. His parents never had a TV set in the house. They didn't have TV in their days, and they turned out fine. There was always something better to do. Ricky was the youngest of the bunch, coming six years after his brother. He was smart, precocious, and always gorgeous. The family had high hopes for him, but something somewhere just went wrong. He turned into a selfish, obnoxious little twit.

Despite Ricky Rutledge's "very, very wrong" nature, he still picked up the family's love of fine culture. He picked up all the Brahms and Bach his parents played on the stereo, picked up on the Greek myths they read to him, he read the complete works of Sophocles and the histories of both Herodotus and Thucydides by the time he was fourteen. He loved his art, but couldn't seem to do any on his own that was worth a damn.

So holding back years of tears, he swallowed his frustrations and became an accountant. He got a scholarship to the University of Missouri–St. Louis, a low-cost commuter college, but with no aspirations this was plenty. This also meant he didn't need to leave home, which was fine for him even though his folks were hoping for a different outcome.

They wanted him out, and putting up with another four years of his bad piano playing, silly love poems, and verbal promiscuity was more than they could handle both spiritually and socially. Ricky knew it, but that's how he was—stumbling through a life of numbers when he wanted feelings and sounds, never quite satisfying anyone in the family, never quite finding the right cookie cutter cliques and societies to force himself into.

The best art he could ever come up with was carving his body. He still goes to the gym about three or four times a week after work. After sitting still in the office doing all that high level adding, subtracting, multiplying, and even dividing, and making all sorts of money for doing it, he gets over to the gym about four thirty for an oasis of time to himself between the job and the marriage.

He can do just about anything by now, after all these years. His endurance, muscle tone, everything, is A-1 perfecto. The stomach is flat, the biceps huge, and everywhere there's a muscle to be seen, you can see it. Just right, not too big, not too small.

He loves every minute of it. The sit ups, the weightlifting, feeling the burning in his arms as he throws those pounds over his head. It feels so good to hurt. Just to feel. His favorite is the stair machine. He can do all that aerobic stuff for an hour at a time, and he's up to two hundred and fifty flights of steps on this little gizmo that imitates a staircase and can take you to the top of the Sears Tower without you leaving the room.

Flight after flight, heartbeat into the groove, longing for the sweat running off him like water, cleaning out all the poison of the business day. Falling down his forehead, over his eyes, drips and drips off his nose, down from the back of his neck, all over the stair machine. His grey workout shirt gets so wet you could wring it out, his armpits a Caspian sea of sweat and steam.

He's the hero there. They all watch him, admiring him. The men want his looks and the women want his body. Everyone wants his stamina. Drip, drip, the whole damn thing's wet now, and Ricky always gets turned on that someone else would be tromping through it. Some guy who can only dream of looking like Ricky, let him slosh through it. Let him swim in it. Fuck, *let him drink it,* it's all I have to give that they want.

It's torrential, rolling down his face, down his back and his chest. Two hundred floors. *We can do another fifty. I'm not tired, not tired yet! I know it'll work.* The ritual cleanliness of the ancients. Take a look in the mirror. He's got a right to be proud of his body. He worked to get it. And he knows they want him. All the women and probably half the men. Some have asked, but no, he's married. *Sorry, but if Emma Williams ain't your mom, I ain't your man.*

Finally it's over. His heart will race for awhile, breath fast and furious, a few more drops off his face to sparkle the gym floor. He's got to walk to slow down, towel off his face. The shirt's a total loss for the day. Just can't wait to get to the locker room to get it off. They won't let him take it off in the gym. Don't want anybody to be showing off too much, particularly if they got too much to show off. How much is too much? More than anybody else, that's too much. When someone gets results everyone else wants, it's too much.

Ricky's dazed as the shower falls over him and the day's work goes down the drain. Quick wash of the hair, quick eyes around the shower, any guys in here worth seeing? Always felt that way a little, but still wants to go home and fuck his wife into a frenzy. Feels spent, exhausted, on top of the world.

Ricky gets home, and it finally kicks in. He eats dinner. Sometimes Sonia's got something cooked for him if she's been home, sometimes he makes it himself. It's always home-cooked. His mother indoctrinated him against TV dinners long ago. Then he's got to sit for a couple hours and recover. It feels good, too. The body feels used, and he can feel it all

42

grabbing up what it can to rehabilitate itself for the next time.

Sonia can't stand it because Ricky won't do anything. He won't fix anything, won't go anywhere, won't clean up the dishes. He just puts on an album and sits there feeling himself exist. So she gets mad at him. He's finally ready to help out, and she's over it. "I did it myself."

"Well you know this is what I do!"

"That's great, Ricky, and I've got to run the whole place by myself."

"Well what do you need? I'm ready."

"Nothing, now." And why bother, anyway? What's the point of having the hot husband with the great body it he's too tired to join the marriage? She flips on the TV in another room and calls a few friends. Ricky stays in the living room working over his glass coffee table, writing his bad poetry and listening to Chopin ballades. Sometimes he wanders over to his electric piano and tries to play them himself. It never sounds as good.

Long about ten o'clock he's feeling a few oats and wants to go sow them in the bedroom, and but now doesn't want to. She's given up for the day. Now she's supposed to turn it on by command after he's pushed her aside for the last four hours.

"This is the way I am," he says.

"Well, change," she says without looking up. "Work out all you want, but I need a husband more than one night a week."

"I'll be a husband now," Ricky says. He licks his lips like a cat going for a can of tuna.

She hates it. "Forget it."

He waits until she's asleep and pounds on himself mercilessly, wishing he could be there with her, to hold her, make love to her, touch her the way he used to, have her admire his looks and physique. All this damn work for nothing.

43

He loves Sonia more than anything he can think of. Known her for six years, married for three. Met at the job when she was an intern from the business school. She was so willing to learn, improve herself, shake off the hateful hoosier legacy of that out of date bungalow with windows always closed and furniture still full of dust from a past generation. Just didn't want to be like her brother. She wanted society, wanted knowledge, wanted friends, dammit! And wanted Ricky to love her. Now Ricky's supposed to love her no matter what. It's just a given. Maybe once a week or so she says yes. Passion drips off him like the sweat onto the gym floor. The bed's sopping. He needs to make love while he has the chance, because he never knows when the next time will be. And she likes it.

God dammit, if he didn't care, it'd be one thing, if he came and went, so to speak. But he loves every part of her, analyzing her like the study of a good poem, line by line, piece by piece. She could never give it all back, never. And she's good when she puts her mind to it, but it's always such a struggle. Sometimes he feels like crying in the middle of the work day and can't figure out why. It dawns on him, maybe he got married anyway so he didn't have to deal with this 'guy' thing. Another stain on everything he's done wrong, a stain the family would have to wash away with even more ostracism.

Seems Sonia agrees with the rest of his family. Deep down, he's a jerk. He doesn't *feel* any different. Maybe he *is* a jerk deep down. *So much to express, and I don't know how. Damn, I'm sorry, Sonia, but you knew what I was like.*

Friday, Ricky took her to the theatre. She'd never even been to a theatre before she met him, but now she likes it. At least likes being there. He can't figure out if she likes the show or just the atmosphere. But he's got to dress to kill, because you just don't go to places like that without looking your best. Right? That's what *her* mother always said. His mother, too, but he was more willing to piss off Betty than Sonia.

Back when he was twenty or so, Ricky scandalized both his parents by going to Powell Symphony Hall in blue jeans. Blue jeans and that chest hair poking out the top of his shirt like grass on an unmowed lawn. *Nobody's paying to see me. I'd rather be comfortable. I can't imagine Mussorgsky would give a shit! I just want to sit and listen.*

Back in Russia years ago
St. Petersburg awash in snow
All the women look their best
Their men work just to buy the dress

All that matters, what's on top
No one cares what else you got
Modest, at night, it all comes off,
Is Boris really Gudonov?

Silly, but they got the point. Ricky never won a poetry contest either.

* *
*

Sonia and Ricky live on Craig Court, in a mess of apartments in Creve Coeur, a reasonably ritzy and reasonably Jewish suburb of west St. Louis County. Ricky is fascinated by Jews. A society within a society that doesn't need to spend four months out of the year preparing for Christmas really titillates his pagan sensibilities. Anything his family doesn't stand for, he'll bite into.

45

It's a nice condo, not too big, and with their double accounting income it's furnished pretty well. Dark green sculpted rug, plush deep blue velvet couch with two chairs to match. The ever-present glass coffee table in the middle. Ricky's always leaving things there. Sonia gets tired of it, but he never mentions her tossing all the mail over the dining room table—whatever she doesn't lose before he gets home.

Saturday night, they're both getting ready to go out, but not with each other.

"I don't know why all four of us don't go out together," she says.

"I guess because we don't want to do the same thing. You're going to a gay bar, and your homosexual brother and I are going to a straight bar."

It did sound funny, now that she thought of it. "It just seems like we never go anywhere together."

"We just went out last night."

"But we're a couple. We should spend more time together."

Well, that sounds like an option. "Let's spend a little time together right now." Ricky slinks up to her and unzips the back of her dress. It's always an inopportune time.

"Ricky!"

"Sonia!"

"Stop that!"

"I thought you wanted to spend a little time together. Just want to make sure you see those gay boys ain't got nothin' on me." He starts to kiss the back of her neck, and she likes it, but not now. She told Tim a certain time and she's going to be there at a certain time.

"Ricky, I have to get ready."

"Get ready? No one's even gonna notice your ass. 'Cept me. And maybe I oughta grab a piece of it to take with me." So he grabs her kind

46

of playfully, and she whirls around to face him.

"Ricky!" It's no fun anymore. "I have to get out of here."

"So do I." A slammed door, squealing tires, and she's alone.

Almost going out together, Ricky and Sonia pull up to their initial destinations just a few blocks away from each other—Sonia to Tim's place on Waldemar and Ricky to Sonia's old house, Castor's place on Bleeck Avenue, south of Manchester, the dividing line between Dogtown and nothingness. Tim's area's called called Franz Park, a subdivision within the larger Dogtown, but nobody really knows it and those that do ignore it. You can't change a century's worth of tradition for the sake of propriety.

Ricky's got the better car, the black Jaguar, and he pulls it in front of Castor's house like he'd done so many times before to get Sonia. Castor always drives them in his Ford. He doesn't drink as much, and Ricky likes to ride in the old car to get a little closer to the real earth.

Castor's been waiting all day. He even does his best to look good, but Ricky likes him no matter what. Doesn't know why, and it doesn't matter.

They always shake hands, like they haven't seen each other in so long. The party was just last week, but that doesn't count. *This* counts. Their night on the town. So rare and so rebellious for these two stunted personalities.

"We got into it before I left," Ricky says. "I tried to make love to her, but she didn't have the five minutes it usually takes."

Well, there's time later, but don't say it. It might go away... "Sonia, Sonia, Sonia," Castor says. He grabs Ricky's arm. "Ready to go?"

"I am ready to get s-*mashed*," says el Ricko, and out they go to the car.

* *
*

Sonia feels a rustle of anticipation she walks up the steps to Tim's apartment. Hears some music pulsing through the door. And Tim's got one of these gay pride shirts on. 1989. She wonders if she's doing the right thing. She doesn't know this guy, and he likes her brother.

"Well don't you look nice!" he says.

"Am I overdressed?"

"No. Wear what you want. This's kind of a uniform for me. Some girls up there, they look stunning. Even the real ones." Tim takes her inside to show her his music equipment. His keyboards, his studio. He plays her something he's working on. Half a song, really. About Castor, but he won't say. Most people can't figure it out. Those asses over at Magnolia's who've inspired his best stuff don't deserve to know.

"This is really neat. How could you afford all this?"

He hates to say it. He doesn't want her to feel sorry for him, doesn't want to go through the whole story. Maybe he should have met her at the door. But maybe he should tell her, to even the score. He knows her husband's been cheating on her. And he can't say a word about it, but it sticks to his mind. "I kind of inherited it," he says.

"Musta had some rich relatives." She's nice, but you can tell she married money.

Tim takes her all over the place at Mag's, giving her a tour and showing her off like fine art. He takes her to the front bar, the back bar, the restaurant, the café, the drag show, the upstairs, the little rooms in the back with the video games, and the patio on the second floor. She's

48

astounded. "This is so neat!" she says. "And the guys are so amazing! They're so handsome!" Some are, some aren't. You just weed a little.

She's a hit. Tim knows all kinds of people and they treat her real nice. Her red dress is down to about her knees, low cut in front, a couple gold chains, three inch heels, blonde hair done up nice. Stunning. Even the guys notice it. And she's got to be straight, to look that nice.

"My boyfriend's sister," Tim says.

"Where's he?" someone asks.

"Out with her brother."

"Why isn't he with you?"

Good question. "Cause he isn't! Castor doesn't like gay bars."

"Oh, Timmee, give it up. It'll never work."

Blasphemy. Someone's always got to break up every relationship you've got. Somehow. *It'll never work.* "No wonder you don't have anyone. You're always saying it'll never work."

Sonia buys drinks for about five guys. She's got the money and she's having a pretty good time. Being treated as a person, letting loose, and she finds it easier to talk to someone she doesn't know at all. A little about Ricky. *Damn, he wanted to—and right before we left.*

"I'd've done it," Tim says.

"Yes, but it doesn't take you two hours to get ready before you leave the house."

"And you don't have to douche," some guy puts in.

They dance a little. She can't move around a heck of a lot in those heels, but it's okay because so many people are on the floor you can't do much anyway. Just sort of sway back and forth like sweaty convicts in an overcrowded prison.

Everyone's real close, trying to be polite, not hit each other, not step on each other, not knock anyone's drinks off the railing. A few aren't so polite. A few arms flail into faces, a few hands fall into the groin. That's no accident. You get that everywhere.

And in the middle of all this masculine mayhem, the dream finally comes back, the little electric tambourine, the drums, the drone, the high notes, pounding away just like anything else. Tim turns around to see Chuck, who smiles behind his thick mustache and waves. A few more people crowd the floor. "This is *good!*" Sonia says. "What is it?"

"I wrote it."

"No!" Happy disbelief.

"Yeah!" He's really gettin' into it, gettin' down as they say.

"It's great. That you singing?"

"Uh huh."

"You didn't tell me they were going to play this."

"Thought I'd surprise you." *Now shut up so I can concentrate.*

She hugs him when they're done. Tired and sweaty, they go off the floor, back upstairs where it's a little quieter. Dale's up there, someone a little more familiar. Dale thinks Tim's taken to this family too fast, but it makes sense since he doesn't have one of his own.

It's about midnight and a half now, and Tim looks to Sonia to see if she needs to leave. It's okay, because he can be back in thirty minutes.

But no, she says. Why bother? Ricky won't be home 'til tomorrow anyway. She gets herself a Coke. It's all different upstairs. More real. Somehow you can talk about your life up here. Not downstairs. Here, there's no reason to escape. Her escape is Tim's face. That he listens, talks back. She can tell her deepest secrets to a stranger. Tim's used to it. Sonia's a little too repressed, but here, it's okay. Here on Planet Magnolia, her ship touches down, and she can anchor and let her worries get off the boat and visit the port. So Tim gets a one sided view of the Rutledges: Ricky, Dave, Ted, Betty, the whole clan. Life is good but it's still hard. *I know Ricky's gorgeous, but you don't know what he's like.*

"You should see this chick's husband," Tim says to Dale and a couple others.

Sonia brings out a picture. They marvel, pass it around. "You lucky bitch," someone says to her, almost hatefully. Sonia takes a sip of her Coke and munches on a few peanuts. Shells on the floor, like everyone else does.

If they only knew.

Castor and Ricky are in the Ford, pulling out of Castor's driveway. Castor takes a glance over at Ricky's perfect profile, glistening in the lights from the moon and the street, shining in the window and reflecting in the glass. He reaches over to hold Ricky's hand just for a few seconds or so. Unspoken affection is always okay. Ricky's not stupid.

Pull out of the driveway, down the highway, the high of this sought-after companionship makes the ride fulfilling, conversation or no. Sometimes with Castor, it's a no. Ricky's used to it.

"Birthday time," Castor says out of the blue.

"Whose?"

"My baby's. Two hunnerd thousand. Take a look."

Ricky peers into the lights of the odometer—199,999.6 and getting ready to turn. Maybe not a lot for a thirty three-year-old car, but it sat for a bunch of years.

"Hey Castor, you did it! Let me take a picture for the mental camera." Ricky cheers it on and Castor blows his horn as they ride down Highway 40 toward the Landing. Ricky grabs Castor's leg for a moment.

"I know there's two hundred more in 'er!" Castor says. Little things like this, who else can he share it with?

Ricky's preference for classical music makes some of the bad downtown bands just a little better than intolerable, but Castor likes the country rock stuff most, and Ricky puts up with it to achieve his ultimate goal of semi-debilitating inebriation. Castor's got the formula down pretty well: get him drunk enough so he'll put out, not pass out. Get him talking. Castor likes the sound of Ricky's voice. It always sounds happy. Strong and in control, better than his own short, smoky utterances. Ricky talks about his job, Castor about his job. Ricky hates his, Castor loves his. And Castor never went to college. Turns out Ricky's company prepares taxes for Castor's company. *See, we do have something in common!*

A few beers for him, no big deal. He drinks beer all the time, and Ricky only when he goes out. So let him pig out. Let him ogle the ladies. There's plenty of good looking ladies for him to ogle. Plenty my ass. They're everywhere. *If I liked women I'd be here in a flash.* Castor just thinks of himself as liking men, not not liking women. It's just the way he turned out.

And Ricky can drool over who he wants to. He's faithful to Sonia on all counts. A man doesn't count. It ain't another woman, just something different. Something he can't get at home. He's got all the rationale together by now. And nobody knows anyway. Not even Emma.

Castor has to get Ricky back to the house by twelve thirty or one, while they're both still awake. If he misses the chance, it's usually another three weeks before it happens again. He can stand the three weeks well enough, but not the missed opportunity. And he needs to show Ricky how he feels. He just can't say it. He has to show it. Has to touch him to get it across. A new idea for him. It's never been this strong before. It's not even revenge on Sonia anymore, it's Ricky, only Ricky, the only one in the world who can make him feel like his miserable life is worth hanging on to, like it's worth doing something with rather than waiting it out down the highways of south Missouri and Arkansas.

A great time that night, loud music, getting a bit rowdy, walking through society finally feeling like a part of it, back on the way home. *We knocked 'em dead!*

Man, they was lookin' *at you!*

Into the driveway, Ricky's had enough beer, and he's pretty turned on by all those chicks. And by Castor. *No, it's not even men, it's just Castor. Just 'cause he's a friend. That's not really true, but that's what I'll tell myself tonight. I'm too drunk to argue my own logic.*

Castor looks at Ricky on the other side of the car. Says, "Ricky!"

"What!"

"Just..." He pulls Ricky closer for a kiss. Ricky's never kissed a man before. Castor's never attempted it. It's the last thing you do with a straight guy, touch his lips with yours, grab the back of his head and hold him to you, feel the release of passion deep down your throat. That's not sex, that's feeling. "...that!"

Ricky smiles, jaw locked open. Powerful, full of beer breath, tongue, and mustache, and no escape. "That's nice."

Castor looks into the steering wheel. He can't let Ricky see how happy he is. Can't risk losing it.

He used to think of his sister, but now she doesn't cross his mind at all. Just an afterthought. Just the reason this can't happen all the time.

Ricky thinks of his wife. She's dancing her heart out at Magnolia's. Wonders if she's thinking of him. But Castor does all sorts of things Sonia won't. It's pretty much the same every time, but then Castor isn't that creative. Still kind of nice.

Castor puts him down on the bed, rips off his shirt, going after Ricky like a dog for a squirrel. Kisses his neck, his chest, his armpits. Sonia won't do it. *I'm not sticking my tongue through all that hair.* He remembers that real well. It was pretty funny at the time, but not now. Now that someone will do it for him.

He'd been faithful to her for the whole six years. Quite an accomplishment, considering his looks. This Castor thing, it's like a buddy thing. A guy thing. He doesn't really see Castor or himself as gay. Just feels awful good. Kind of a cement on the male bonding process. Castor really makes sure Ricky is *sat-is-fi-ed.* Castor will feel all his body, reveling in it, in all the work Ricky puts into it. Ricky's appreciated—finally. Castor doesn't care about a rubber, either, but Ricky'll use one because it's his upbringing to be considerate.

Castor never lets guys fuck him anyway. He doesn't care for it, doesn't see where being gay means sex has to hurt. Except for Ricky, he'll deal. To feel Ricky possess him, drip sweat on him, watch him lose himself in lust and know it's because of Castor. It's what Ricky needs, and Castor knows it. He knows his sister won't do it. Get down and dirty. Get all about the sex. *No fucking way on her part.* And Ricky's getting into it more and more. He just doesn't see Ricky as straight, that's all. No matter what he says.

Ricky feels it's a fairness issue. It's not right he should lay there and let Castor do everything. Just payback. Felt odd at first, touching a guy that way and tasting male flesh. But he remembers Sonia's cry about not running her tongue through all that hair, and he decided to be better than that. And Castor likes it. He likes Ricky's spit all over him. *God, Ricky, you are hot!* When's the last time he heard that at home?

Castor knows Ricky's falling for him. Knows it. Knows sooner or later Ricky's gonna be his man. Like about now. Ricky grips Castor's chest like a vice. It hurts so, but it feels good. If Ricky feels good, it's okay. The rest of the world subordinates itself to Ricky's sex drive. Castor knows it.

A blood rush to his head, a twinge of guilt, euphoria, just like climbing up two hundred and fifty flights of stairs, Ricky reaches the top of the Sears Tower. Maybe twice. Castor follows, not far behind. Then Ricky falls asleep. He's an athlete. He sleeps well. He can feel Castor holding him in some unconscious part of his dreams. He feels comfortable, feels like someone really wants him there. Castor feels at home. His heart is at rest. Wants to take Ricky to Little Rock with him, have him in a hotel. It's all finally together. This warm body of a gorgeous man, maybe too good for him, but Ricky doesn't seem to mind.

Ricky wonders sometimes if he married the wrong Williams. *No, maybe not. This is different. If we were together, we'd fight just the same. Let's keep it at this. Something good, something quiet, something awful I can never take out of this room.*

Sonia comes home after three in the morning. She's had a great time. She's tired, and she has a headache. Drums through her mind. Coke, peanuts, *you don't have to douche,* the music's so loud it's still hard to get to sleep. She falls exhausted into the empty bed.

Ricky showers in the morning and gets on home. Not even a kiss goodbye.

Tim comes by Sunday and has Castor pop in a tape of some Danish disco. Some musician friend sent it to him from Copenhagen. Tim can't understand a word of it, but it sure sounds neat. Right?

"Sure, Timmee." *God, so many gentlemen callers. It's like* The Glass Fucking *Menagerie in here.* Something Castor learned from Ricky. Some play about sad people in St. Louis.

Tim's getting into his Danish disco, but really he's scared to death. Afraid of last night, afraid of Castor and Ricky alone in the bed. Look, the sheets are new. *Well, it is Sunday.* "How'd it go last night."

"Great. Turned two hundred thousand on the Ford."

"Neat! What'd you all do?"

"Oh, drank. Walked around. Ricky likes them women kind, you know. Came back here and went to sleep."

Tim's getting all over Castor again. The hands, those hands go everywhere. Sometimes it gets to be a bit much. Sometimes a guy just wants a little peace, rather than a little piece. It ain't that big a deal if he gets laid every night of his life. Mostly it's the beer, the TV, and his right hand. Big deal, you know? But it's nice having someone around. He likes Tim a lot, but they don't click on a lot of things. Just in life, they don't click. But it's neat, being admired, so leave well enough alone. And keep the Ricky thing separate. Nothing's going to happen with Ricky for a long time. So let it go.

Tim wants to ask it so bad. *Did anything happen?* But he won't. *But if Castor says no, it means he likes me, no matter if he did or not.* Tim tries not to play the possessive game after so short a time, but he's ready to settle down. It's stupid, but that's how he is. "Sonia and I had a great time!" he said.

"Really? Good. I didn't think she liked to have a good time."

"Oh yeah. She's a lot of fun."

"Well, you can take her out all you want."

56

"Must have been tough growing up here," Tim says. Sees that's what Castor's getting at.

"Yeah."

"What's up? You can tell me. I don't have any family. You can tell me anything."

Castor shrugs. "Yeah. Tim...Tim, I need a little space, okay? Just for a little?"

That usually means good bye. Forever. "You want me to leave?"

"No, just sit in a fucking chair, Man, I like you, but I need some space."

"Okay."

It's like putting the dog in the corner. How do you say it's okay? Castor doesn't think of it much. He just knows if Tim stays in the bed, he'll sock him a good one. "Sonia 'n' me were so different. There wasn't enough room in the house for both of us. And mom really pushed her. Said, 'you can make something of yourself. You're smart.' I wasn't smart. I don't know why, I just wasn't. So Sonia got good grades, went to college, met Ricky, got married, turned her back here. And Dad left earlier, so when Sonia went off, it was too much for Mom to take. So, now I'm her son again."

"You think it's kinda odd, living at home?"

"Where else you want me to go? She can't do nothin'. Can't take out the garbage, can't really clean up. She can't even get to the fuckin' bathroom sometimes. I don't know how much more she's got to go. She just sits here and watches things happen. You know she bought that ball o' yarn in 1988 to make Sonia a sweater, and it ain't done.

"But I really like to drive, Tim. I love to drive. There's a lot more to it than you'd think. Havin' a truck behind me, anyway. I...I really like bein' alone in my truck, you know. I like bein' alone, Tim...and..." *God, it's the whole Ricky thing backwards.* "I don't wanna mess with your head. I'm the way I am, and I don't wanna be any different. You're looking at me like there's something in here, and there's...just, this is it. You're gonna get hurt digging. You're gonna fall into a real deep hole. I got nothin' to give you but this here room and these beers."

"You're so down on yourself." Tim's got to discount the whole thing. "Maybe I see more in you than you think is there." The tape snaps off loudly, one of those old stereos you can't fall asleep to because the cassette mechanism is too loud. Tim can't see turning it over right now. "It only really takes one person, you know, to like you." He wants to say *I love you,* but it's too soon. Wants to go back to the bed where Castor's laying, but it's too soon.

"Everybody's down on me. It don't bother me anymore, you know. I'm just over it. Your family died, yeah. Mine just walked off. You see me with any friends? Ricky's my friend. And they all think he's stupid for likin' me. Well, I'm glad you're around."

"It's no problem." Maybe not. Usually he'd be at Magnolia's by now. Sunday night's a big night at Magnolia's. "You wanna go to Magnolia's?"

"No."

"It's a lot of fun. You oughta try it. Sonia and I had a real good time last night."

"Then call 'er."

"You don't have to go looking for a trick."

"You can go if you want. I won't be hurt."

Tim stays in the chair. He might not see Castor for a few days as it is. Castor's gone the whole middle of the week truckin', and if he gets more work, who knows when he'll be back around. He's told Tim he tries to keep it short so Mom's not alone too long. But Tim's a night owl, and he'd talk, make love, or just go out for all hours when Castor's putting the lights out at about eleven-thirty. It's an early day of getting the truck loaded up and heaving it around the city. Or out to Warrenton, or something like that. *Out to some shopping mall, I think.*

So he isn't in the mood to get laid, *but yeah, Tim, it's okay to spend the night.* And Tim feels a little better, because he sees it's his company and not his tongue that's getting him the points.

Tim gets into bed in this outdated lonely room. Clean sheets, anyway. He can touch Castor again. It seems silly to be in the room and not touch him, not take advantage of it.

Tim can't sleep for a long time because his schedule has nothing to do with going to bed at eleven thirty. He's a little bored, but still where he wants to be. He should stay here while he has a chance. Finally falls asleep with an arm around his man. Big warm hunk of sleeping man. Castor pulls him closer during the night a couple times. Tim's in love, and he's scared.

A note in the morning:

> You were sleeping and I
> had to go. I'm busy tonight.
> See you Friday, drivin' til then.
> Castor

Emma sees Tim in the morning, pouring himself a bowl of corn flakes. They've said it's okay for him to do that. Another means of validation. He can be there by himself.

"You know, just between you and me," Emma says, "Castor's a strange bird. We're kind of a strange family."

"All families are strange." *At least you've got one, so shut up.*

"I just don't want anything bad to happen to you, hangin' around us."

"Thanks."

"Castor's never had anybody over here as much as you come."

"I've only been here a few times."

"I know. I'm kinda happy for him. He's just not used to being... loved."

Just an impulse. "Why don't you make him a sweater?"

"Castor?" She smiles a little. It never occurred to her.

CHAPTER 5

Ricky tries to make friends at work now and then. Have someone to go to lunch with who can make intelligent conversation. Usually he just eats in his office and listens to his portable CD player.

Lots of women would kill for a chance to eat lunch with Ricky Rutledge. Those who wouldn't kill for it would probably die for it. So he asks Norma Jade Smith, who he perceives as reasonably intelligent, to go to lunch because he wants a little company. No big deal. The diamond on his left hand shines bright enough, so there's nothing left to the imagination. Or maybe everything left to the imagination.

Norma Jade doesn't understand the point of lunch from his perspective, but she likes the view. She'd be happy to sit there all afternoon and study the angle of his nose jutting out from his face, the square-up of his jaw, the promise of his body under his shirt.

But that's inappropriate, so she talks about work. She talks about her boss, her clients, asks questions about some accounting problems. Ricky makes more money then she does, so surely he knows what to do.

Yeah, I can tell you how to fix it. But wait till we get back to the office. Domenico Scarlatti's *Cat Fugue* starts playing over the Muzak, an old friend in an unfamiliar setting, a jazzy arrangement of it by Bob James, but Ricky doesn't know who did it. It grabs his attention after all the faceless music he's heard so far. *"The Cat Fugue,"* he says.

Norma Jade doesn't know what he's talking about.

"The music. That's Scarlatti's *Cat Fugue*. In G minor." Not so much to impress her, but just to get it straight in his mind. The Cat Fugue *on the Muzak. There is hope for society after all.*

"Oh," she says. "I don't listen to that."

"They call it *The Cat Fugue* because people used to say it sounded like a cat was walking across the haprischord."

"Well, yes, it does," she says, but she's not impressed.

Ricky's rather impressed with Scarlatti. *Did she know that he wrote one harpsichord sonata about every three days for the last three years of his life? Not bad for a guy who was seventy two.*

"That's very interesting, Ricky." Good looking men are always interesting.

No it's not. He can see it a mile off. He can smell it in her perfume. "Sorry, I guess I shouldn't drag you out to lunch and start talking about pussy."

Norma Jade wishes to hell he *would* start talking about pussy, but because they're in a work environment, she doesn't feel she can ask. Worse yet, she feels proper protocol demands she act offended and tell Ricky not to broach the subject again. Otherwise she'll be called a home wrecker, and they'll fire her because Ricky's higher up. If Ricky's not watching her ass, she needs to do it herself. So, Ricky's back to lunch with the CD player. He gets this idea for a *Cat Fugue* video, with this animated cat walking across the piano and making all sorts of funny faces while someone's trying to play the music. It takes him over, and he can't get any work done the rest of the day.

Tim spends the week counting down the days—Monday, Tuesday,

Wednesday, Thursday, Castor's busy Monday? *Busy? What the heck could he be doing? He never does anything at all. Wonder if it's another guy. Can't be. He's got me.*

Dale's visiting up in his apartment, and Tim's giving him the whole Castor story, rehashing and rehashing until Dale can hardly take any more.

"Look," Dale says, "if you're gonna date a trucker who drives over the long haul, you're gonna have to face the fact that he's gonna be gone a few days a week. Some truckers are gone a lot longer, and they have a good time out on the road. If you don't like it, get someone else."

"I can't find anybody else. And I don't want anybody else."

"Then write him a song. You can't hibernate four days a week."

"I *am* writing him a song. I don't know if he wants to hear it, though. I don't know if it's his type of music."

"Get a job, Tim. You're so bored."

"Dale. It's not boredom. I just want something to come from this. I've never had it. That love thing, never had it."

"Maybe it's not time."

Tim's defensive. It's always time for love. "It *is*. It just makes me nervous."

"Isn't it amazing how we're always so unhappy when we're in love?" Dale's sprawled out over a chair and Tim's on a couch, shaking a foot back and forth with uneasy tension. He moved over the family furniture from the house, and he can still remember playing board games on it with his brother and sister. He'd get new stuff, but he doesn't want that memory to die with them

Dale's got close-cropped hair and a thin beard and mustache with a welcoming smile. He's Tim's "Black best friend" from the apartment below. He came and went as he pleased most of the time. It couldn't have been any more convenient if it were a TV show. He's a medium framed guy, maybe five-nine, pleasant enough to look at, for sure. People always suggested he and Tim get together for all the time they hung around with each other. Dale's body print was indelibly beveled into the chair. But he's heard Tim talk about man problems enough that he knew better than to get involved. He usually leads his own much milder personal life out of Tim's shooting range.

"I don't think Castor's ever been in love," Tim says. "This might be something new to him."

"*You're* the one who's in love. He don't sound like it to me. He could probably take you down to Little Rock if he wanted you with him. Or wherever it is he goes."

"What am I gonna do in a truck for three days?"

It would be better for Tim if Castor would drive out over the weekend, but usually that's when he's back home. You never know what his schedule will be, but such is the life of the man who trucks to please. Unfortunately, weekend dates with Castor cut into his Magnolia's hours. He knows so many men who say if they would only find the right guy, they'd never go to the bars again. Then they meet a guy who goes out until three o'clock every night and wonder that he won't stop after they become lovers. Tim doesn't want to stop. His whole world, his society, his friends, are all there. He wants to bring Castor in, to share him with the multitudes, to show everyone that he has the *hot* guy. If Mag's ever closes, Tim will be lost.

But he really likes being with Castor. He gets a feeling he never gets from anyone else. Castor hasn't based the relationship on his looks or his talent. He doesn't know what it's based on. Maybe just that he goes there and Castor doesn't have to do anything.

The next best thing is Sonia, so every now and then he calls her up just to see what's going on. She's usually not busy because Ricky's not coherent enough to occupy her time. She wants to go to Magnolia's again. Maybe she'll wait until Ricky goes out with Castor, maybe not. If he can do it, then she can do it. *Maybe we can do dinner or something during the week.* Since Ricky works out and Castor's gone. Yeah, second place and second place. But what the heck, right? It's all there is.

So, Sonia's at his apartment one evening, and Tim brings out the scrapbook. Somehow wants to share this mess with her. She saw the family picture on the wall and asked about it.

He's got pages and pages of stuff about it, about the crash, the trial, letters from Mothers Against Drunk Driving asking him to speak for them. *I wouldn't do it, not to be a poster boy.* He kept it all just in case he'd need it for something.

"I always wanted to be on the front page of the paper," he said.

Sonia remembers it now. It was quite a news story at the time. The quadruple killing. "Yeah, things float around for awhile and just go back where they came from."

"Not for me. It's still floating around."

"It must be horrible to live with that."

"It hurts. I see people complain about their family all the time. I don't even have one. The aunts and uncles, you know, they don't count."

"Didn't they take you in, sort of?"

"I'm gay. So, no."

Sonia knows a little what he's going through because her father disappeared when she was fifteen. "We never knew what happened to him. Castor woke up and found the keys to the Ford on his dresser. No note, even. Castor loved that car, and I guess Dad wanted him to have it. But after he left, Castor went into this little shell and never came out. He was really pretty quiet even before. No one could ever get through to him."

"What'd he go for?"

"Nobody knows. Maybe just us. Livin' in that house, too small. Me and Castor never got along, Dad and Mom never got along all that much. One day he was just gone, and he never came back. I don't know if I'd want to see him again, or what I would say."

"You feel kinda lonely sometimes."

"Yeah. And Ricky. I don't know where that's going, either. Sometimes things that are fun before you're married aren't so much fun after. So, yeah. Lonely." She's lost in her own thoughts: Dad, Ricky, Castor— all the important men in her life, all of whom had let her down.

"I feel it all the time," Tim says. "I know friends are a lot more important to me than to other people. And love. My friend Dale says it means too much to me. I try to say he's wrong, but I know better."

"Ricky's folks have a big family thing. As I guess you saw. They say family is everything. Without family, you are alone. And they keep it together. No matter who they have to kill."

"I really love Castor," Tim says. He can't say it to Castor, so he tells Sonia. "He really means a lot to me."

"But you barely know him."

"I've known him for awhile. And when you spend time with someone like that, just alone with them, you get to know them pretty well."

Sonia doesn't know what to say. She doesn't want to be the black sun that puts out Tim's world. "Well, Tim, I've spent a lot of time with Castor. That's why I don't do a lot of it now. I don't think he knows how to love. I think you could be beating your head against a brick wall. He just never...never *was*, that's all I can say. I wanted to have an older brother I could look up to, but he would never look back."

Tim has this mental vision of him and Castor in bed, the passion, the goo, the smiles. *Can't love? Bullshit.* "He can. He just can't say it to anyone."

"Trust me, Tim." She sighs again, can't figure out how to get it across. She knows she's got bad press all the way around, knows Tim's divorcing her from her family so he can be her friend. Now she doesn't have any credibility in the field, even though she's the specialist. "I know you don't like hearing this, but there's something wrong with him."

Tim finds himself looking at her face, trying to see if there's a resemblance between her and her brother. Maybe a bit. Their looks are as different as their personalities. "People get along differently with their families than they do with outsiders. So you have a different impression than I got. It's hard to shake how you grew up with people. Well, not that I'd know."

Tim's flipping back through the scrapbook, back through the sentencing, the trial, the arrest, the aftermath, and the accident. And all that money dropping into his life. "The guy who did it got twenty years, you know. Four counts of vehicular manslaughter. Drunk driving as well. Couldn't get him on murder." He's ready to cry. Twenty years of what most of his life was, wiped out by one drunken Carl Buggs. Carl looked at Tim in the courtroom and burst out crying. He was only twenty years old, too.

He closes the book and Sonia says she better go. Ricky might be coherent by now. Maybe they can rescue some quality time together before the week's out.

Tim spends his weekdays creating songs, trying to come up with enough really good material for a dance album. Maybe even make a

CD. So what if dance music isn't the world's biggest seller? It's what he likes. Trying to write really good songs, good lyrics, good music, avoid all the rat traps of bad relationships he's been writing about. He brings Dale up to hear everything and ask for opinions.

Now he writes about Castor. Music in a style that Dale would like, lyrics that might bring Dale closer to him, he writes for Castor who couldn't care less. He loves Castor, and Castor's good to him, but he's still scared. The security isn't there. Sonia and Ricky hate each other, but they've got security.

Tim hears the call of the train passing by a few blocks from his house, near the old Scullin Steel plant on Manchester that went out of business ten years ago. It lays out a mournful jazz chord when it chugs by. Lately it's been more cacophonous than ever. Sometimes it comes in right in the middle of a vocal, throws the whole thing off. Castor's house is even closer to the train than Tim's. Some mornings there, it's almost like it's going to drive through the window. Castor says he hardly hears it any more. After thirty five years, it doesn't ring in his ears much at all.

Tim's working on something like:

If you let yourself love me
I can show you heaven

But he's not quite sure. It sounds clichéd. And he doesn't want to get into the Stevie Nicks groove, where she sings lyrics promising that only by loving *me* can you find happiness. And what rhymes with heaven? *Seven, eleven, unleavened... We'll have to fix it.*

Phone rings.

"Hello?"

"Tim?"

Vaguely familiar voice. It's always a thrill when it's an unrecognized man. "Yeah?"

"Hi, Tim, it's Ricky Rutledge. Remember me?"

Doesn't click in for a minute, and then...!!!!!...it might as well be The President of the United States! "Hi Ricky!" *Of course I remember you. I've jacked off forty times thinking about you.*

"Hi. How're you?"

"Pretty good." *He couldn't have called just to talk.* Tim doesn't know what to do with Ricky. Ricky's violated the marriage principle. He's cheated on his wife. And his wife has become Tim's friend. And Ricky's so damn desirable, he wonders if he wouldn't have to cast Sonia to the wind if he had the chance. All these thoughts, and Ricky hasn't even said anything yet.

"Hey, look, Sonia was telling me you're a musician?"

"Yeah."

"She said she heard some of your stuff, and it was really good."

"Yeah. Good. I'm glad she liked it." He's tongue tied. Even over the phone.

"Well, this is a long shot, but you know...I write stuff. I just thought maybe you could see if you wanna...use anything." It *is* a long shot for Ricky. Everyone hates his poems.

"Well, maybe."

"Why don't you come over and take a look?"

Tim's eyes bug out. Castor or no Castor, spending a little time with Ricky? Can't be denied. "I can come over now."

"I'm working now. Hey, Sonia's gone Wednesday night. She signed up for this class. With her job. Some accounting shit. You'd think she got enough during the day, but she wants to learn more and get a promotion. Come by about seven? I don't want her to know. I'd like it to be a surprise, if you can do something."

Tim's so dumbfounded. What if Ricky's calling just to seduce him? Damn, why's he thinking about sex? Just an innocent phone call. He's made hundreds himself to get his music out there, and maybe one in a hundred gets a lick. He kicks himself, can't get over it, though. Well, he's heard so much about Ricky, maybe it's time to see for himself. Just make sure to wear jeans.

CHAPTER 6

All the love I have for you
Binds my fingers up with goo
Thinking thoughts a man should hide
When his libido ranges wide

Why's it when I see your eyes
I want what floats betwixt your thighs
To lay you on a bed supine
And probe the depths of your vagine

"Vagine?"

"Poetic license."

Ricky's got Tim on the couch looking through his volumes of poems, paging through notebooks spread out on the coffee table. Some of them go back to 1972. Just brought them all out for effect.

"Ricky!"

"What's wrong, you think it's too heavy?"

"Vagine?" Tim repeats himself. He laughs a bit. So tasteless, yet so amazingly... tasteless.

Ricky closes the book, laughs at himself. "I never showed that one to her. She might think I thought she was pretty," he added quietly.

Tim's amazed. This man who everyone's been talking about one way or another, here he is as creative as can be. Sadly so. Perhaps badly so, but his poems have a wild imagination to them, if only they can be controlled. He doesn't know how to say he can't set it to music.

"I wouldn't feel comfortable writing...*this* stuff. You know, singing it. But work on something new, listen to what's being done, and I'd love to." He can't throw away a collaboration with Ricky just like that.

He's having a dilemma. Sitting next to Ricky, he can't gaze into his face, but if he moves to get a better view, he can't touch him. Can't brush against his leg or rub against his fingers or any of the other accidental friction that might happen when they turn a page.

"That'd be great," Ricky says. "I think it'd be real neat. I'll see what I can do." Here he is looking at Tim, ten years younger than he is, from a whole different world all together, but he's *doing something*. No family to disapprove of his ideas, maybe.

Ricky thinks Tim's awfully cute. He's experimenting with this idea of bisexuality. Doesn't know how it fits, but it seems inevitable. Women are still his main drag, but every now and then... He's got to figure out if it's men or if it's just Castor. And he can see the admiration Tim has for him. It's a different thing coming from a man. A whole different ball game. A way of separating the carnal from the spiritual, that we can just fuck each other's brains out and still only be friends. Something like that. He's not really sure. It's bothering him, and he's taking it out on Sonia when he shouldn't be.

Ricky takes in the shock of seeing his lifetime of out on the table. So many years, so many pages. He never realized there was so much. So much past thrown in here. Tim's the first one to see most of it. Sometimes Sonia would page through it here and there, but she couldn't take much. Couldn't figure out why Ricky would write it down. *Just keep a diary, you make everything rhyme. Life doesn't always have to rhyme.*

72

I remember dear Sonia
(Which rhymes with begonia)

Did you know that you can't say "iambic pentameter" when writing in
iambic pentameter?

There once was a poet named Bill
Whose girlfriend made him quite ill
He wrote in pentameter
The better to have at 'er
But she wouldn't give him his fill.

Shakespeare, of course, but Tim knew that. Just a few doodles, nothing serious. "But I will do it," Ricky says. "I need to. I've been wasting my life on shit nobody cares about. Other people's money."

Tim scoots down to the end of the couch and turns sideways so he can look at this wonderful creation that Ted and Betty Rutledge bestowed upon unsuspecting humanity. *He cheats on his wife.* The "Ricky's a jerk" theme keeps coming back like an obnoxious pop song that won't go away, but he can't see anything too jerky about the guy, just that he's supposed to be. *Gosh, what would I do if he...*

Ricky looks back. Their eyes meet for a few moments, but Ricky breaks it. It's too fruity. *He knows my wife. He'd probably fuck up my marriage, but then I could ruin his life in three minutes.* "Yeah, I will do something." He says it again. He doesn't know what else to say, but Tim's saved the evening because he brought a tape of some of his stuff. About thirty minutes worth, so they can listen to it for awhile.

It doesn't matter to Tim if he's got an audience of one or five hundred, as long as someone's listening. He'd produce a song just for Ricky

73

to hear if he asked. Just to know that somewhere somebody cared what he was doing. Just to know he wasn't alone.

The phone rings near the end of the last song, about the worst possible place, because Tim's afraid the call will cut off any praise he gets out of this. And he knows Ricky's bound to be complimentary, since they're collaborators. *Yeah, let's collaborate. And do some songs, too.* It's so damn hard to keep to the subject at hand when everybody in the world is a possible sex partner. But Ricky's different. Ricky's a dream. It won't happen anyway. Think of Castor being hurt. *Yeah, right.*

Ricky's talking to his mom. A few perfunctory comments, and the tape runs out. He puts her on hold for a minute. "That's great, Tim. I'll talk to you about it in a bit." And he goes back to Mommy while Tim's left on the couch with nothing to do but look through old volumes of Ricky's poetry.

And even that's taken away from him. Ricky closes it all up and puts it in a pile. He kicks back, stretches his arm out over the back of the couch and puts his bare feet up on the coffee table. *Yeah, even to see your feet, your toes, just something that's yours, that'll keep me interested.* Tim hates when people talk on the phone and leave him hanging. It's rude, not to mention a real bore.

Ricky's wearing a yellow pullover and some jeans. He even came back from the gym a little early because Tim was coming, because it was someone to talk to who knew about creating. He beckons for Tim to sit next to him, inside that outstretched arm, so Tim turns the other way and leans up against Ricky's body. He closes his eyes just to enjoy his fortune and smell Ricky's after-shower scent. He's close enough to the telephone that he can hear both ends of it.

What do you want to do?

It's almost Ricky's birthday. Thirty four, and Betty wants to make a

74

production. Ricky's amazed she even cares, but maybe it's just another excuse to throw a party. Well, he's got news for her. "I think we should go out. Just you, and Dad, and me, and Sonia if she wants to go. Just go eat somewhere nice. I don't think we've ever done that. Not since I've been married."

But I already told everyone we were having dinner over here.

"You didn't tell me."

Well, that's why I'm calling you.

"So if I don't go, everybody's gonna have my birthday party anyway."

That's what it looks like.

"I don't understand. You asked me what I wanted to do." But at thirty four, he's not going to beg his mother to spend time with him.

Tim's pretty comfortable. Ricky smells really fresh, a combo of soap, shampoo, and cologne. Maybe it's something the rich folks do, use cologne just to stay around the house. Or maybe Sonia likes it. Ricky finally gets hold of Tim's hand, plays with his fingers, but the whole thing seems really unsure. Tim loves it and feels shitty about it at the same time. As long as it's happening, he might as well enjoy feeling it. Hairy guys are his thing. And strong hands. Ricky's hands aren't big, but they're sure powerful. But it shouldn't be happening.

"I wanna bring Tim and Castor."

And his mother, I suppose. A sigh. She should be banned from West County.

"It's my mother-in-law. She never does anything but go to your house. She's probably too traumatized to go anywhere else after a night with us."

Well, enough of this shit. Ricky says goodbye. He's over it. Puts the phone down and lets go of Tim. They both feel the same way. *Sonia would puke if she found out.* So would Castor. Ricky gives Tim a quick

75

look which says, *I could have you naked in the bedroom in three minutes.*

And Tim's look says, *It'd be great but we can't. Now drop it.*

Ricky starts to realize that male-male contact is never talked about. "Damn my mother does the same thing every time."

"What's that?"

"Acts like she gives a shit. She's got the whole family coming to wish me happy birthday." His hands conduct his words like they're a double forte in a Beethoven symphony. "And they don't. Even. Like. Me." He takes his books and puts them back in the bedroom. "Well, Tim, I guess you better go." *And leave it alone.* "She might be back soon. But I'll be in touch. And I like the tape. You're a creative guy." Pop music's pretty much all the same to him, but he knows diplomacy. God knows how; he didn't learn it at home. "Oh, and cool fingers."

Maybe he won't leave it alone.

Tim's got this weird and sick feeling about Sonia and Ricky and Castor. It would be better if none of them knew each other. Better for him, anyway. Better if he could just appreciate Ricky for his scattered way-out mind rather than obsess over his never-ending good looks that made it so easy for everyone to betray everyone else. *Well no, I didn't betray Castor. Not just by leaning on someone. I just used him as a utility pole, that's all. Then I went home and beat off three times.*

But he's looking forward to Ricky's birthday party, because, even if the whole Ricky thing is wrong, he's kind of wondering how far will this go with no persuasion on his part? And he's still trying to figure out what everybody thinks Ricky's problem is. Other than he's a manipulative cheater.

The first order for party prep is to make Castor more presentable. That 'Goddam Rutledge Outfit' would wear pretty thin after repeated use, so Tim's going to use some of his disposable income to dress up his man. And to get him out of the house. Saturday afternoon doesn't seem like the time to spend inside with the blinds drawn and the TV on watching senseless old movies and bad cable commercials. So we do this by degrees.

We take him down to South City where he'll feel more comfortable. Before the clothes stop, Tim's got another surprise in store: the Boggs '50s Emporium. Down on Cherokee Street, Antique Row. Take Grand Boulevard south to Cherokee and go east for a spell. When you hit Jefferson, you're at the end of the strip. There's stuff there from just a few cents to seventy five hundred dollars. They rely on the slumming traffic from the county. Nobody who lives anywhere near Jefferson and Cherokee could afford seventy five hundred dollars for some Victorian vase. Unless they were rehabbing, maybe.

But Boggs might be fun, because it's all the stuff Castor's got, and he might like to see it for sale. See what people pay for it now.

J. Greggson Boggs is a big wheel in the gay community, in more ways than one. He's about two hundred and seventy pounds, not pretty, has a boxy nose, thin mustache, and light brown hair, but nobody really cares. Wears round wire glasses too small for his face, smokes incessantly. He works with gay pride week, makes political statements, and occasionally threatens to run for mayor of St. Louis.

But people like him. And he's got a pretty nice lover. His friends call him Greggs, and they say it's because he's so big that one Gregg just won't do. He's got all kinds of stuff, even the front of a Fifties Impala in the window. Tim's fascinated with it.

Castor's seen this shit every day of his life. Mom and Dad never had

77

money to get new furniture, and Castor wants to spend his on some-thing else. He doesn't know what yet, but certainly not furniture. *All you do with a couch is sit on the damn thing, who cares what it looks like?* And certainly not this shit.

Tim thinks it's so neat that there's a Fifties antique store in town. He never thought of the Fifties as old before. Tim knows Greggson a little bit, just from being around, from some gay activities and the bars. Everyone knows who Greggson is. "This is my friend Castor," Tim says. You don't say lover here, or boyfriend, just in case someone might be scared off. *Right.*

Boggs looks out the window. "That your car?"

"Yep," Castor says.

Boggs is delighted. Wow! "That just fits right in. How much you get it for?"

Castor doesn't know. He was only two. "Uhh. 'Bout a grand."

"You're kidding!"

"No. Why would I be kidding?"

"That thing's got to be worth ten or fifteen thousand. It's in perfect shape."

"Yeah." Castor smiles a bit. *What a dildo.* "Got it new." So he plays along a little bit. Goes looking though the drinking glasses for sale, the pictures, the furniture, like it's something real neat. And the lamp in the corner. The one with the fish on it. "Hey, Timmee." He beckons Tim over there. "We got one of these, don't we?"

Tim's in euphoria over the *we.* "Yeah. In the living room."

"Got all this stuff," Castor says.

"Castor's whole house is Fifties," Tim says, excited, because maybe Castor and Greggson have a common ground.

"Got it all," Castor says. "Got the lamps, got the table like that one, got the pictures. Timmee's the only thing I got that ain't old. Mama bought the stuff once, and she kept it up."

"I'd like to come by sometime, see what you got."

"Don't see why. It's the same shit."

"Maybe I can get you a good price for it."

Castor's a deadpan here, and Tim can't figure out what he's going to do. "You want me to sell it?"

"If you want!" Greggson is still in awe of the car, maybe a little of Castor's demeanor as well. Yeah, a trucker. You don't even have to ask. Just kind of a cool man.

"Then what am I gonna use?"

"What do you mean?"

"I mean, if I sell you all my stuff, then what am I gonna use?" Castor's got a bit of an Arkansas drawl coming out here.

Greggson's confused. "Well, you don't sell me what you're gonna use."

"Well then I don't got nothin' to sell ya.'"

Greggson's getting a little afraid and he doesn't know why. "Oh!" It dawns on him. "You mean, it's just in the house. I thought you had it stored away."

"I don't got no room to store it away. Me and Mama, you know, we're real functional like. You're treatin' all my shit like some kind of curiosity shop. Outta here, Tim. Out, out, out." And to Greggson. "I don't have to junk my car and then buy the same goddamn thing thirty years later at ten times the price."

"I'm sorry." J. Greggs is still confused. Tim's embarrassed as shit. Doesn't know why. Castor didn't raise his voice. Didn't raise a hand. Just seemed to get so upset over nothing.

"Just messin' with him," Castor said later.

"No one thought it was funny."

"I didn't either. You know, I'm proud of what we have at home. It's all I got in my life to be proud of. It ain't much, but we kept it good. We never had any money, and one thing my mama taught me was not to fuck with what you got. And I come in here, and he treats it all like it's freaky or somethin'. And he wants to make money offa me. I don't wanna be like one of those fuckin' new age freaks on TV like I'm something weird. It's just my life."

"It's okay, Castor." Tim's a little afraid, too. A real dark mood.

"It *ain't* okay."

"Okay, then. It ain't okay. You're right."

"Wow, when'd that happen?"

Tim takes Castor's hand, questioning his own validity.

"I know you didn't mean nothin' by it, Tim." Castor rubs his hand down his face, his way of making the world go away. Like pressing the clear button on a calculator and starting all over at zero.

"Let's get you something to wear, then." Tim forgets that when you get involved with people, eventually they stop being perfect to you and become themselves. He's hardly ever been so far along with anyone. Once people start being themselves, he usually has to duck out. But this time, maybe he can stay. It's weird, but it's good.

So into the modern atmosphere of St. Louis Centre, the downtown mall that was supposed to bring all sorts of people shopping where they'd never shopped before. Downtown! *Yeah, right.* You can get to the same stores in the county, without the Black kids.

Tim's trying to find something trendy that'll look good on Castor.

He's got to remember the guy's thirty five, not twenty three. Look at him. He's tired, worn, washed out. He's got that damn cigarette. *One pack a day? Tell me more lies!* He's got more of a pallor than a complexion today. His hair looks dull, and his mustache reminds Tim of Tchaikovsky. Bright colors will just bring out the pale and make him look like a mortician's workload.

So Castor winds up with the faded look: a vertical striped blue and cream shirt and some faded jeans. Tim gets him the expensive kind that are faded just right, a little light blue and a little white. Castor walks out of the dressing room, and Tim wants to take him right back in to pounce on him. "Take a look."

Castor in the mirror. Yeah, he does look good. Tim opens a button to expose a little more of his chest. "Right!" He's in his glory. He's done his man up right. Gets Castor a little leather belt with some studs on it.

Castor feels a little like a statue, the way Tim looks around him and through him, but what the hey? What does he know about what's in, anyway? When you're in a truck, no one can see what you're wearing. *Besides, Ricky might like it.*

"When we get home, I'm gonna take this shit right offa you," Tim says.

A little later, they're sitting on a bench in front of the yogurt place at the front entrance of the mall. Lots of plants, lots of elevators, lots of people. It's so gay! And not in the homosexual sense, either. Castor says, "You really wanna buy this for me?"

"Yeah." Tim's a little quiet. He's putting himself on the line. "Just want to get you something. You've done so much for me, feeding me and keeping me over. I just like you Castor. I just wanted to show you. I've wanted to for a long time."

"But it's eighty dollars."

"I'm worth a half a million. Insurance. Yeah."

"Five hundred grand you can't get to."

"Well, you look great, and that's what counts." Pause—three beats to the wind, wait for the beat to pick up. "You can say thanks if you want. That's what I was kind of hoping for." Maybe *I love you*, but let's not push it.

"Oh, sorry." Castor's pissed off, and he doesn't know why. "Thanks."

"Castor, are you okay?"

"I ain't in my truck, I ain't okay."

"You got your car here. Hey, you want a yogurt?"

Hand down the face again, but it's the same tragedy when he opens his eyes again. "Tim, I ain't used to you. I ain't used to anyone. I'm not used to all this trendy stuff. You know, the music, the clothes, the friends. I felt like a fish fuckin' out of water or something."

Maybe a fish out of fucking water, or a fucking fish out of water. Castor's using fucking as a verb rather than a modifier, but Tim doesn't bring it up. "You got Ricky. He's pretty trendy."

"Ricky ain't the same thing, okay?"

"What's the difference?"

"I don't know. Maybe..."

"What is it?"

"Maybe...Tim, I don't know..." A little irritation. Not really at Tim, just at the world by now.

"You want me to hang around still?"

"Yeah." No hesitation. No great alacrity, but at least no hesitation.

"I'll try not to mess you with things you don't wanna do."

Castor nods. "Okay."

But Tim doesn't understand. He just wants to get Castor out of this self-dug hole, into the world, into *his* world. Maybe he'll have to

82

drag Castor kicking and screaming, but he'll like it once he gets there. "Castor, I love you."

Castor gets this feeling of warmth and fear, but the warmth overtakes him for now. He's never heard it before. "Let's go," he says quietly.

* *
*

Back at Castor's place, both of them still reeling from Tim's confession. Tim figures Castor really needs some sensations, so to speak, really to be touched, to feel how much Tim loves him. Tim didn't expect it would be said back to him. He just had to get it out. Let the chips fall where they may. A really hot time might put him in a better mood for the party. *Yeah, right Castor. I'll lick you till we have to wring you out. I will, I will, I will. I just wanna hear you moan. That's all I wanna hear outta you.*

"Ohhhhh..." Castor replies.

If you let yourself love me
I can show you heaven

And even if you don't. Tim makes mincemeat out of Castor's whole body, buying a little time, thinking he could spend his whole life doing this and the music. How could anything else even matter now? Greggson is gone. The St. Louis Centre is gone. A stroke up Castor's thigh... closer, closer, *I've hit paydirt!*

"God!!" Castor involuntarily invokes the deity.

Tim gets this idea he's going to suck the guy off until he spurts in his throat, and he sets down to work it out. He knows it's stupid, *but hell, Castor hasn't been with anyone. Trucker, trucker, yeah. My trucker!*

Castor's so lost in it he almost forgets who's doing it. He knows somehow that it's wrong, he's leading a lonely young man down a rocky cliff like a siren leading him to his doom, but it's so hard to say no. So hard to stop it. It's so damnably wet and perfect. He could never throw this kid outta here and give this all up after so long without. *I've gotta be clean,* he figures. *And it's not my problem anyway.*

Castor growls, he gnashes, he twists his lip, Tim almost chokes on the result. He doesn't know what to expect. It sure ain't a Hershey Bar, this slimy goopy mess running him down from all sides. But Castor likes it, *and perhaps in my miserable little life if I can make him happy for these few seconds, at least I'll have accomplished something.*

Castor just lays there with his mouth agape and eyes closed, blood rushing around his head, finally coming to a stop. Takes him a while to recover. Hell, who wants to?

Tim makes himself swallow the whole load, just to have part of his man with him. No one he knows ever died from swallowing it. Hopefully.

Castor finally looks at Tim. Tim shrugs his shoulders. The smile goes, replaced by a tight mouthed look of regret. *Once on the lips, forever on the mind...*

"Tested negative anyway," Castor says. "Got scared once, and I came out okay."

Did you like it? Say something!! What a shitty ending to such a hot experience. And Tim's been messin' with the guy for an hour. *Castor, do something.*

Castor's spent like the last dollar before payday, but a deal's a deal. *Thank you.*

CHAPTER 7

So, it's party time. Tim and Castor look more matched this time around. Like a couple. Even Emma's amazed. Castor looks so good, she barely recognizes him. His clothes actually fit and flatter. But Castor feels kind of weird. Those jeans look like clouds. Oh well. Think Ricky. Ricky wears this stuff sometimes.

Tim, Castor, and Emma are sitting in the living room passing a little time. Tim walked out of the bedroom in an after-sex daze and somehow it was only about three o'clock. All that shopping around didn't take that long. Maybe the sex didn't either. Emma has that look on her face of "no, I didn't hear anything." *Sure.* He notices her ball of yarn is a little smaller. Since he made that suggestion, she's been knitting away slowly, fighting off the cat who keeps pawing at her strings of yarn. Maybe...

Ricky's been preparing a little more creatively. He hasn't talked to Tim in a while, but he's been diligently working on a song that might work in the hyper-emotional field of dance music as well as get a point across to Sonia. It hasn't been easy for him.

I wonder if you love me
The way you used to do
I remember all the nights
~~*We'd stay at home and screw*~~
I'd make sweet love to you.

The fifteen-year-old in him just won't go away. But after some hard work, he's finally come up with something pretty decent about wondering where the love went and maybe it's still there if we look hard enough, that kind of stuff.

I wonder if you love me as much as I think I still love you

That's all you need. Why did it take him all day to come up with it? So for once, he's looking forward to one of these awful parties, but only because someone in the world cares what he's written. Can't share it with Sonia, can't share it with Castor, and the family is a big never mind, *la gran nunca mente* as he once said wrongly in a Spanish class, so when it comes to his pent-up creativity, Tim is all he has. Maybe that's why Tim's looking so good lately.

The tulips at the Rutledge house have been replaced by irises. They're next to the house, along the walk, by the driveway—blue, purple, yellow, orange, bolstered by some annuals planted by a landscaper. It looks like Shangri La. Tim's got a long time to look at it because it takes Emma a few minutes to get up the walk. Maybe she'd be better off in a wheelchair, but she won't give Betty the pleasure.

Ricky's already at the door waiting, his two favorite men arriving at the same time, the sexual and the creative outlet right before his very eyes. Which one is which is a bit of a blur. Ricky looks awfully good today, like there's a time when he doesn't, but now he's got his hair cut short on the sides and spiked on top, and it makes him look like he's about twenty five or so. Maybe because he's getting older.

Castor remembers Ricky some mornings with a hangover: unshaven, tired, and his hair randomly out of place. It's his biggest turn on. A handshake, a hug, Sonia comes over to say hi as well. Tim feels at home, even though Ricky's parents have yet to address him personally. Well, they don't address Ricky much either. But all the family's around, presents are on a small table—like there's something Ricky doesn't have—and Tim sees a cake in the kitchen. Quite elaborate, with a little piano on it. Ricky's seen it too. *Like they care.*

Ricky's immediate challenge is to get Tim away from Sonia so he can show him the lyrics. It's been on his mind all day and after a bit, he corrals Tim into his old bedroom and locks the door. Tim's about to lose control here. The fantastic nature of this little journey is tickling his sensibilities.

Ricky takes a folded paper out of his wallet. "I didn't want her to see me give you this, is all. I just think it'd kinda be neat for her to hear it later," he says, thinking of how damn cute Timmee looks while he's talking about these lost love lyrics. *Well, dammit, if she'd really love me, I wouldn't care about Tim one way or the other.*

Tim scans the sheet over, thinking of a little tune. He works fast when inspired. Yeah, he wouldn't even work with these lyrics if Ricky hadn't written them. They're okay. Nothing great, but great lyrics aren't a priority for today's dance hits.

"Good, Ricky. I can see some feeling in here." He meets Ricky's eyes for a moment. "Sorry that you had to write it—I mean, that you feel that way."

Ricky rubs his hand through Tim's hair. "Yeah," he says, real quiet. "Real sorry." He gets sad for a moment, lost in thought. All this garbage casts a foul odor over the song. For a minute, he kicks himself for dabbling in the world of men—messing with Castor, messing with Tim's head. Yeah, he can read Tim like a piano sonata. It's the old trite problem of being loved for his looks, at least on Tim's part. Castor's different. And Sonia? *Well, she deserves it.*

"I can get some good ideas for this," Tim says, breaking the spell. "I'll get right to work on it."

"Thanks. It means a lot to me. I know it isn't much."

Tim wants some attention for his own creation. "What you think of Castor's outfit?"

"Looks good. I've never seen him that way."

"I got it for him today. He fought me on it, but I wanted him to look good for tonight."

"Well, ain't you a tasty Timmee." Meant tasteful, but *whoops!* Maybe.

"I got this stupid costume party coming up. I don't know what I'm gonna do," Ricky says. "Sonia's going as a fairy godmother. She's got a bridesmaid dress, and she's putting in some sequins."

"I bet she'll look great."

"We've defied tradition. She's wearing a bridesmaid's dress twice." Ricky finds that funnier than anyone else, ever.

Tim takes a look at Ricky's face and dark hair. "I bet you'd look good in leather."

"Leather? Right, Tim."

"It's a gay thing, but I bet you'd look real good." Tim's always been

88

fascinated by guys in leather, like they had some inner mystery he could never solve. But once he got behind the façade, they were just like everyone else, except perhaps with a tint towards the painful. "Let's do it! Get you some chaps, a harness, some chains... You'd *be* the party."

"Maybe you can help me out. I don't know anything about it. I've got this problem with creativity. I want a lot more than I have."

"I'm pretty trendy. I can dress you up real nice."

"I'll let you know."

Pounding on the door. "Ricky are you in there?" No answer. Fuck them. "Richard! Everyone's waiting to eat."

Ricky rips his shirt open and unlocks the door. "I don't know what happened, Mom. He took me in here and started tearing off my clothes. I protested, but to no avail."

"Ricky, get out of there!" Mom's mad.

"Tim, you devil!" So, he walks into the dining room buttoning up his shirt while Tim's sticking the song lyrics in his wallet and adjusting it in his jeans. The whole house is suspicious. Castor's inflamed. He's ready to bust some skull.

He calms Castor. "Just messin' with my mom," he says. "Tim and I are working on a surprise for Sonia. Writin' her a song."

Yeah? I got a surprise for Sonia! Castor thinks.

And Ricky's not done messin' with his mom. He waits for everyone to sit down at the table and holds up a wine glass to the light, fingers clutching the stem.

"Ricky, what are you doing?"

Ricky's pissed. "We can't eat here."

"What is your problem tonight!" Now Ted's in on it, too. All this work for his benefit, and they're rewarded by Ricky being himself.

He looks from his glass to the others, serious as a conductor starting Mahler. "There's spots on the glasses. I come all the way out here to celebrate my birthday, and there's spots on the glasses."

Tim thinks it's funny, but nobody's laughing.

Mom doesn't pick up. "I washed them before you got here."

"You didn't use the Cascade, did you? You used it for Dave's birthday. I just get some plain label Aldi's shit for mine. Always the black sheep. Baa."

"If it's not good enough for you, you can go home and we'll eat," Mom sort of gets it, but she's not playing along. Dad isn't either, and neither of them are opting for dignity, which would be the only way to salvage the wine.

"I'm sure the food will be just as delicious without you," says Ted. "Even more so, without your rancid conversation to ruin the flavor."

Ricky catches the star in Tim's eye, shining just for him. *Finally, someone who understands.* But he's screwed up the dinner. Not only did he say "shit" at the table, but the relatives were scandalized. Some got the joke, but they were shushed by the others. Betty's glare signaled that no one was to play along.

Damn, Ricky figures, if *he's* seen it on TV, then everyone else must have, too. The rest of the family *watches* TV. Everybody knows Cascade gives you dishes without spots and the bargain brand is... well... a wash. He just wanted to see how it would play out in real life. It *can* ruin the dinner if you make a big enough stink.

Tim grabs Castor's hand under the table. Silent acknowledgement between the charter members of the R.R. fan club. Castor's really happy because Sonia's madder than shit and won't speak to Ricky all night.

If she does, it's pretty simple. "Pass the salt."

"We gotta do the Landing, Ricky," Castor says.

"Yeah, looks like we do."

90

"I'll speak to you."

Betty decides she'd better sweep Ricky's antics under the table or the whole evening will be a disaster. My God, he's thirty four now and look at him. Never could grow up. *How'd he ever get a job? That's right, we got him the job.*

So she pours the wine, spots or no, and Ricky gets the usual birthday amenities: the cake, the presents, even a little bit of attention, but with Sonia in such a snit, people are afraid to talk to him.

He corners her in the kitchen trying to get her to smile, to be his wife, to take his side.

"Sonia, I was just having a little fun."

"I guess you and I don't have the same idea of fun!"

"No, I guess not. I like to fuck and you *don't* like to *get* fucked."

She's over it. "Oh, why don't *you* get fucked!"

"Why are you so into playing my family's song? I'm your husband. Try standing by me for once."

"It was embarrassing and uncomfortable. Kind of hard to stand by that."

Ricky walks to the big room at the back. Castor's standing near the patio door eating a piece of cake, wiping icing out of his mustache and sucking it off his finger. "A walk on the patio?"

"Let's go. I feel like trash."

"She did it again?"

"Yeah, Castor. Was it that big a deal?"

"It was kinda funny. Not fall on the floor funny, but funny enough."

"I like your clothes."

"I like your hair."

Sitting on a bench out by Betty's fountain and fish pond. Look around at dark flowers. It's night now. Hardly any words. None are needed.

"Well, happy birthday, anyway."

"Thanks." Grabs Castor's hand. Castor shivers all over. Tim's *I love you* runs through his mind. Maybe he can use it here? Maybe not.

Unspoken feelings and fish, all there is to think about. Colored lights behind the fountain: red, yellow, green, blue. Must be a revolving light, like on an aluminum Christmas tree. There's one been in the Williams's basement for years. No one brings it up anymore.

Watching the fish is just like trucking. So calm and mindless. Get lost in it. "You oughta come down with me to Little Rock sometime."

"Maybe I will." Ricky replies, but he knows Castor means it more than he does.

Little Rock's Castor's escape. Of all the cities, that's his favorite. Whatever days he drives, he's away from Tim, Ricky, Sonia, Mama, Morgan's, and his smoky little room. Freedom, the open road, sometimes a stranger, but not since he met Tim. Bring Ricky on the escape? Yeah, sure. Ricky *is* the escape.

Sonia has nothing left to do but complain to Tim. "What were you doing in the bedroom, anyway?" She's got no idea.

"He was telling me how much he loves you."

"No, really."

"Well, in a way, he was."

"I wish he'd tell *me*."

"People tell me things sometimes. Do you ever tell him you love him?"

"Of course I do."

"Well, maybe you oughta tell him again. Right now."

"Maybe I got too mad too fast. My dad used to do that, and I picked it up." So she goes to the patio and sees him sitting with Castor. Calm, quiet, low voices, sharing secrets. *Why can't he do that with me?* It's just like grade school, those two. Sleeping over...sticking together... just...not...right...

The words stick in her throat.

Back home again. "Boy, he really did Betty and Sonia in this time," Emma says. She can't do it, so she's glad someone does it for her.

Tim laughs. "I think he did us all in."

"Yeah." Castor's horny again, and he's not so sure why after just having had sex this afternoon. Probably because of this evening. Tim'll oblige. *I like Tim, really.*

Tim's getting ready for the lonely week. Monday night is Castor's last day in town for a while, and he always keeps that last day to himself. Says he just needs the time. He's used to being alone and he likes the feeling. He gets things done around the house. Got to shop, take Mom a few places, get some groceries.

"I'll help."

"Please, Timmee."

"Just seems silly that I can't be with you."

"A lot of things are silly. You and me, that's silly. Get a life. I got one. It's the only one I have. So I can't give it to you."

Monday's a shitty bar night, and he can only spend so much time in his studio. If Castor wasn't a factor, he'd find something to do. Everything else seems second hand now. He's got friends. Lots of guys would just take him out to dinner to try their hand. When you're twenty three and that hot, guys will buy you dinner every night of the week just for the privilege of looking at your face. Don't even need to take you to bed.

But that doesn't matter to Tim anymore. Castor matters, and Castor's gone so much and so often. Who knows what he's doing?

Tim tries to take his mind off it by working on Ricky's song, thinking about Ricky—another lost and stupid cause, especially since Sonia's such a close friend. What is with Ricky, anyway? Leading on his wife's companions. He loves her? He really sticks it to her. And who can resist him? He never talks about his looks, but it's always the most important part of the conversation. It's a lose-lose situation there. The whole thing is lose-lose. Emma keeps telling him to get out. It's a mess. Trust her.

"I gotta trust myself."

"Well, don't you go trusting anybody else. They won't come through."

Dale's been hearing some thump-thump disco through the floor and comes up. The door's always open. Tim doesn't have a bedtime. Dale does, but he doesn't care. He pulls out a group of four photos from a little booth at the mall. Him and a bigger square-faced guy named Darnell smiling and making funny faces.

"When did this happen?" Tim's happy but he's not. He always feels Dale should stay single in reserve.

"We've gone out a few times. Cool guy. He likes me, I like him. That's about it for now." It's not, because Dale wants to talk about Darnell for the next hour and a half. Tim owes him for all the nights he's gone on about Castor. The difference is that Dale is upbeat and Tim just complains.

"When do I get to meet him?"

"Maybe this week if we're still together," Dale says with a chuckle. Gay relationships aren't known for their longevity. "Maybe we could double-date sometime."

"That'd be great!" *Other than...* Tim shrugs. "Other than Castor wouldn't go."

"We too Black?" Might as well put it out there, Dale thinks.

"No. Nothing to do with Black. Just with people." It would just be too much trouble and would end badly, and it makes him mad to think about it.

Castor's a little mad too. Why won't Tim just give him some space? *Quit smoking, go to Magnolia's, go here, go there, I want you every minute you're in St. Louis.* Too damn much. Well, don't think about it now. Keep your eyes on the road.

Castor's been driving for about three hours or so. It clears out his head from the rest of the weekend. Get lost in the lane markers, the cars looking like little ants on the pavement, smile at the other truckers. Sometimes they smile back. *Yeah, male bonding, what do they know?* Once or twice he's had one follow him to a rest stop. Cab's so damn high no one can see. Maybe more than once or twice. Maybe a few times. Who counts?

Castor had to get it on the road because he never went out in St. Louis. He didn't get into the bars. Didn't understand why being gay was such a common denominator that all those people should gather together in one spot, so he got good at plowing Missouri's back roads,

unearthing a man here and there who'd be into the same thing. Sometimes guys would want to see him again, but it wasn't a big deal.

You'll be back in a week or two? I could meet you.

Maybe. I don't know what I'll be doing.

What else would you rather be doing? Winks smiles, tongues, zip-
pers.

Driving.

Yeah, the sex drive was there, but not the feeling. Never let go to
admit you need someone enough. Not till now, and it really hurts. Goddamn sister got everything. Got the money, got the education, got the
looks, got the man, and she treats it all with such spite. *If I had it, I'd
use it right.*

WELCOME TO
ARKANSAS!

Big shit. Drive on. Country station playing softly on the radio.
They're hard to find sometimes in the middle of Styx. His eyes catch
a body, a thumb, and a backpack. Some young guy's hitching along the
side of the road. *Good, I need it. Take my mind off my life.*

He slows down and the guy runs up to the truck.

"You know I'm not supposed to take people in the truck." He always says that.

"Well, thanks," says the guy, climbing up next to him.

"Going to Little Rock?"

"Little Rock. Yep."

"Yeah," Castor says.

"Where else is there to go?" It's Little Rock or nothin' for this one.

Castor thinks out loud. "Fayetteville. I got to go there, too. But Lit-

96

tle Rock first. Kind of a short haul. Maybe Dodge City if there's a load for me. One nothin' to another."

"I'm goin' home," the guy says. "Got pissed at my parents and ran off to St. Louis. But we've patched it up for now."

"Well, I can get you home," Castor says, coming to life a little. Conversation's easier with a stranger. "I like this job. Gets me away from everybody a few days a week. By the time I get back, they've all forgotten everything."

"What's your name?"

"Castor."

"Your first name?"

"Castor." He goes through this all the time. Sometimes he lies and says it's Bill Castor, from Williams. It gets old. "Hey, would I make something like that up?"

"Guess not. My name's Tex."

Castor smiles. "No it ain't."

"Yes it is."

"You ain't old enough to be a Tex. Ain't no Tex on earth under thirty nine."

"It's my second name. Matthew Texas Barlotti." He gets his license out of his pocket. "See?"

Castor glances at it. Arkansas Drivers License. Looks so odd, even still. Matthew Texas Barlotti. DOB 12/9/72. *72? God, I'm gettin' old!*

"So, Matthew Tex." Castor's drifting into the Arkansas drawl. M.T.'s got a little of it. After being down here for so many years, it's just something fun to do.

"You gonna show me yours?"

"It's in my front pocket here. Can't get to it."

"I can."

97

"Go for it." *Here we go. I don't even want to be bothered.* Matthew Tex reaches in and pulls it out. What the hey, right?

Williams, Castor Earl. DOB 8/19/55. 6'0", 179. "You're 35?"

"Yep." Matthew Tex tries to fit it back in but it won't go. Castor grabs it and throws it on the seat. "Fuck it."

"I really like older guys."

"I bet you do."

"Yeah. You're hot."

"Think so?" Castor says.

"Real hot."

"Bet you think I'm just the hottest thing on eighteen—"

"Mm, yeah, Castor."

Get a fucking life. "You know, it really turns me on havin' a young guy like you thinkin' I'm so hot. Really turns me on big time, Matthew Tex."

"Good." So, Matthew Tex reaches over to play with Castor's crotch. Just like that. Well, it's happened before.

"Tell you what, Matthew Tex. You don't mess with me, and I don't toss you out the window. Sound like a deal?"

"I thought you wanted it."

"Don't need it. I get enough."

"I can't ever get enough."

"Yeah? That's 'cause you don't get it as much as I do."

"How much do you get it?" He's vicariously excited.

Castor talks slow, leading him on, fantasizing at the same time. "Oh, couple times a day. Couple hours at a time. Yep. I cum four times on a slow day. Hard." *He believes me. I'm twice as old as he is. He'll believe every word.*

"Well, I could do you for a couple hours. You really get me hard. I love your big mustache. It's amazing. I'd give anything to touch it."

Castor wants it, but he doesn't want it. Not one more, not now. It's all or nothing, everyone or no one. "What would you say about bein' friends?"

"What you mean?"

"You know, friends. You tell me what's buggin' you, I tell you what's buggin' me? You got friends, Matthew Tex?"

"Couple."

Castor goes to his wallet and gets out a picture of Ricky. Hard to do while he's driving, but he can manage. Tosses it to Matthew Tex. "What you think of him?"

"Damn!"

"Married my sister."

"Wow."

"What'd you do if he married your sister and came on to you?"

"Well, I mean, it's my sister."

"Well, I know. But he really likes me."

"Is he gay?"

"Hell, I don't know." Not the label. Don't label Ricky as anything.

"It'd be hard to say no."

You probably can't say no to anybody. "I know. I love him." There. The admission. *Someone else knows, and it doesn't matter. Someone out of the world.* Average looking clean shaven kid, half smiles, crooked tooth or two, probably never see him again.

"So what do you do about it?" Tex wants details, if not an invitation.

"I take care of it." Enough already.

"Can I keep this?" Matthew's gaping at the picture, hoping it will come to life.

"It took me forever to get it. It's all I got."

But Castor opened a can of worms about what's buggin' who, so now he's got to hear about all Tex's problems with his mom and dad. Things don't change, do they? Every eighteen-year-old has his gripes. Voice kind of goes on, conversation here and there, second place to the roll of the tires, the hum of the truck, the feel of the road. The radio underneath it all. Little Rock: 50 miles. Stopping in about 40 to unload, reload, a little farther down then to eat; it's an all day trip. Next day to Fayetteville, maybe Bentonville to mess with Walmart, maybe Oklahoma, maybe Kansas, sometimes he doesn't know. He'd go out farther and make more money if he didn't worry about mom, but Sonia won't do it so he's got to. Can't blame her, she's got a new and better life. Who needs the shit and misery she left to rot and die on Bleeck Avenue? One day he'll truck to California and stay there. One day.

Castor talks to the guy without even being aware of it. Kind of soothing, passes the time.

Matthew scribbles down his number on a piece of paper. "Will you call me sometime when you come to town?" Maybe friendship isn't so bad, after all.

Castor takes the number. "Sure," he says. "If I get to it."

"I'd like to see you again. Really would. Even as just friends."

"Yeah, it's been fun." No obligations, no muss, no fuss.

"Just talk if you want, or more. I'm always ready." He kisses Castor on the corner of his mouth, wants to get his lips on that dark blond mustache. Affection, not sex. Like Ricky. No one can see, so who cares?

Yeah, who cares?

Matthew Tex disembarks in Little Rock, Castor feels good. Kinda weird, just talkin'. Almost feels better. No problem. No pain. *Maybe I'll call him.* Yeah, his mama'll love that. Thirty-five-year-old truckin' man from St. Louis droppin' in on her teenager. *Howdy ma'am, I just put the eighteen-wheeler in the driveway. Yeah, me 'n' M.T.'s gonna hit the club for an ice cream. Then he's gonna suck my dick all night long. And ma'am...? There ain't shit you're gonna do about it.*

Get out of my house!

No mom, I love him!

No problem, no pain.

CHAPTER 8

Phone rings early in the morning, about 8:30. Tim's barely awake. Everyone knows his hours. Never call him before noon. But it's Ricky. Ricky's voice could pick him up any time of day. Always sounds like he's in a great mood. And Ricky's at work. He's been up for awhile already. Work...right. Sometimes Tim forgets how the world at large makes a living.

"So where's the best place to get leather stuff, Tim?"

Tim's awake, but not coherent. "Los Angeles."

"I don't think we could make that. What's closer?"

"Chicago."

"Okay. Anything around here?"

"Some stuff. But they'll have more. When do you need it?"

"Next weekend."

"Chicago." Tim doesn't know what he's saying. Like Ricky can bop all over the U.S. of A. "Ricky, can I talk to you a little later? I'm still kinda tired."

"Oh. Sorry about that. Tell you what. I'll take off next Wednesday and we'll go get some stuff, okay?"

"Sounds great..." Zzzzzzzzzzzzzzz.

"Thanks. I knew I could count on you."

Tim isn't quite sure what just happened. Did he make plans to fly to California to get a leather outfit? Dumbshit. You can get one here.

Might take awhile, though. He doesn't even know why Los Angeles came to mind.

* *
*

Greggson pissed him off a couple days ago. When Castor headed for Little Rock, he went back to the Fifties Emporium to apologize. Just to say that Castor usually isn't like that, but he's not the most social of creatures.

"You can do better than that, Tim," Greggson said to him.

"I don't recall asking you for a judgement," Tim said back to him. He was usually cool-headed but he'd had enough of people telling him to dump Castor.

"Well you can. You need someone with a little culture to him. He's just a guy off the street."

"He's my lover," Tim said back. "I believe in him."

"Looked like he was gonna slug me."

"Well, maybe you deserved it." And maybe it was time to dump Boggs Fifties Emporium from his lifetime itinerary. Some people get it into their heads they know everything about everybody. So he spent the week working on Ricky's song, hoping to get it done before Ricky showed up next Wednesday. Wouldn't that be a surprise! It was coming along pretty well. A new kind of funk, for Tim anyway. A little drier, a little slower, but quite danceable. And not too many problems with the words. Nothing blatantly sexual or juvenile or any silly references to female anatomy. Yeah, it'll work. Chuck at Magnolia's won't know what to do with himself. Two hits by local songwriter.

He really pushed himself to get it done, but when things are moving and when airtime is in the offing, it's worthwhile. He's got a Mag's

103

date with Sonia the night after the costume party, so maybe he can get it played for her then. See what she thinks. See if it will restore her floundering marriage.

Weekend with Castor, of course. Stayed in Friday, went crazy, went out Saturday, back to Castor's place Sunday. Not much going on. Mama, a little TV, a little sex. Castor ain't doing it as much as he used to, but maybe that's the way it goes. Tim doesn't take Castor out anywhere this time around, not after last week. Castor tells Tim a little about Matthew Tex. No big deal. *I'll go with you someday if you want.*

Maybe. Tex was easy. I dropped him off. Gotta do my job, don't forget.

Ricky says he's comin' by about seven on Wednesday morning, so get ready. "I got us some tickets to Chicago, Tim. We're goin' up about eight thirty, and we'll be back about six."

"Ricky, we can't do that!"

"Why not? See, I think you and me, we have something in common. I could tell at that party at my mom's." A little zinger hit Ricky right between the eyes during his Cascade tirade, that somehow, *Tim is one of us!* "I think we could use a little vacation. Get to know each other better. Take you to lunch in Chicago. I wanna do this costume up right. And maybe I'll have some other uses for it. Ain't like a bridesmaid's dress. I'm sure you can wear it more than once."

"What else ya' gonna do with it?"

"See if I can turn you on." Real sexy like.

"Ricky, stop."

"Yeah, tell me that later. I'm just messin' with you, Tim. I'm not really gonna try anything." *Like hell.*

Shit.

Tim's in a state of shock. The prospect of going to Chicago for the afternoon and coming home? No one will even know he went.

What's more, no one will even know Ricky went. It's Wednesday, the day of Sonia's accounting class. He told her he had family stuff all day, and she wouldn't want to be involved.

And it's Ricky just talking away. In the car, on the plane...which is good, because Tim's hardly awake enough to say anything. He's seen seven a.m. from the night side, but get up for it? Please. He's a bar man. Full time. Except lately, he's got Castor. Castor and his damned normal hours.

"This's gonna cost you a lot of money," Tim says. "You sure it's worth it for a costume party?"

"Yep. What's the point of earning a living if you can't do what you wanna do? 'Side from that, I'm a Rutledge. If I need something, I can get it. I'll beg my dad if I have to, and he'll pony up to keep me from reciting poetry. You really got it made, boy," Ricky says. "You got money and you don't work. You can do what you want."

"Yeah. But no family."

"Well, me neither. Difference is, mine's alive. They don't do me any good. I'd quit my job in a minute, you know, and live like you. Sometimes I get this feeling I want to throw my whole life away and start over. Especially the family. I wish they loved me, and maybe they do. But we live how we do. If I didn't have to work, I'd go to the gym all day and play the piano all night. Sometimes I just feel like cuttin' loose, you know? Dump it all. Even Sonia. I know I shouldn't say it, cause I know you're her friend and you'll run and tell her, but—"

"I won't."

"Really?"

"Ain't my business."

"Yeah. Remember it ain't. And don't think she wouldn't do the same to me. But you get used to things, and you just keep them. But I really...I have no life. You get to create stuff all day long. Maybe I should try to get more into it. I know if I had time, I'd do better. But nobody gives a damn. Nobody really cares. Mozart, Bach, Chopin, yeah, it's all fine that *they* did it, but not me. I had to be a damn accountant. My parents are so into the fucking arts, and they don't even give a shit that I'm doin' something 'cause I wasn't as good as Mozart, Bach, and Chopin. The MBC combo. Yeah, of course I wasn't. Who is? You know why I like you, Tim? Because you *do* care. 'Cause I can show you something, and you care. I'd just as soon live in a garret and have a piano."

Tim feels so sorry for the guy. All dressed up and nowhere to go. No wonder he's such a jerk.

"I suppose you're really bored by now," Ricky says to Tim. He's wearing cutoffs and a bright yellow t-shirt that says: *To All You Virgins: Thanks for Nothing.* Tim can't believe anyone would go to Chicago in just that. No luggage. Not even any saline solution for his contacts.

"They got stores there. It's a big city."

Plane lands. Forty five minutes plus another thirty of circling the runway. That's the way it is in Chicago. Rent a car, off to breakfast, off to some leather store off the beaten path. Tim knows where they all are because he's been to Chicago before. Just about a year ago, when the leather fascination hit, he and Dale took a Boystown weekend. He tried stuff on, but it didn't look right on him. Ricky's another story. *Ricky'll look good in anything. He'd probably look good in nothing at all.*

So the plan continues. Ricky's deciding what to do with Tim. He knows the guy is like Silly Putty, and he finds his attraction growing and growing because Tim's listening. Listening to every damned word.

And he understands. Got to have some kind of reward for that. And Ricky needs it. Needs to bed someone outside of the Williams family. Just to feel whole again.

Tim watches Ricky transform from a virgin-hater to a hung young leather stud in a matter of an afternoon. *Yeah, Chicago wasn't a bad idea.*

Their first leather store is run by a muscular bearded guy who's as effeminate as can be. One look at the virgin shirt and he cries: "Will you take that thing *off?*" Ricky's happy to oblige. The new thrill of showing himself off to an admiring man gets him going. "That's better. Oooh, that's much better." Ricky's got an empty Citibank card in his wallet just dying for some purchases at twenty one percent interest.

"Usually we have to make chaps by hand, but I keep a few on hand for guys like you. Who need it right away." Looks at Tim. "He your lover? You lucky sonofagun. Both o' you. Boy, I bet you never get out of bed in the morning."

"He doesn't have to," Ricky says.

Ricky finds a pair of chaps that fits. Black leather with metal studs down the side. Bright silver. A bit more expensive, but we want to win the prize. A vest and harness to go with it, dark cowhide mixing in with dark hair all over his body, metal on flesh, the whole get-up. A black leather cap to top it off. Just a few strands of hair sticking out the front, raining down on Ricky's forehead. Perfect. His hair's short down the back of his head, down his neck, kind of tapers off. Guys like the hair on his back. Women think it's gross. Seems that way, anyway. Sonia thinks it's gross.

The shop owner takes a picture. *Don't smile, Ricky. Look at me like you're gonna fuck me. Curl your lip. Let's see that bicep.* Says he's going to put it in the window.

Next place is kind of a bookstore boutique thing. Get him a bracelet. Leather with metal spikes. An arm band. Some chains, one around his neck, one to thread through the harness, one to put in his jeans. Yeah, you need jeans. Can't just wear chaps with nothing. Though some try, Tim says.

Ricky's ears aren't pierced. No fucking way. If God didn't put a hole in it, I won't either. Earrings are out.

Ricky stands in the mirror at the boutique, leaning on the wall, gazing at himself. It's hard to believe. He's transformed. He even *feels* gay. Just a little. The diamond ring glimmers on his finger. Reminders of life. Fuck it.

Tim can't keep his eyes in their sockets. Keeps sighing.

Ricky's fascinated to death. He should be. He just spent hundreds of dollars on the outfit. Plus plane tickets. The prize is only five hundred.

Five hundred?

It's a Ladue party. Ladue's next to Creve Coeur, got the richest per capita income in St. Louis County. Big houses on strictly private roads. His boss is throwing a benefit costume party for the Shriner's Hospital. Likes people who take care of sick kids. He should. His kids are sick. Party costs twenty dollars a person to attend. Plans are for about two hundred and fifty people. The prize oughta bring in some good costumes. Ricky says he'll donate the money to the cause if he wins it. He's a Rutledge. He needs to.

Ladue's claim to fame not too long ago was telling an unmarried couple to hook up or get out. Zoning regulations, you see. Can't live together in a house if you're not related. Well, she showed them. Not only did she get married, she got herself elected to the U.S. Congress.

Ricky takes Tim to eat, still in his leather costume. He wants to get used to it, and he feels so odd. People stare the shit down out of him,

108

but no one's going to dare approach him. *If he'll wear it on the street, who knows what he'll do?*

Tim can't control himself. "You...look...so...fucking...good..."

Over lunch, Ricky starts step two of the plan. Wants to see if he can get Tim in bed. Won't be too hard, really. It's immoral, amoral, not moral. Perhaps that's the point. "What do you think of sex as power?"

"What do you mean?" Tim's watching Ricky's sexy hand take salad up past his sexy red lip.

It's a theory he's been tossing around. He tried it on Sonia without telling her, and it kinda worked before she became such a bitch. "The fact that if I'm making you feel real good, I've got power over you. That if I toss you into bed and start messing with you, and you like it, you're giving yourself up to me."

"Kind of. That's how it goes."

"That if you *really* like it, you can't stop me no matter what. No matter if it's right, it's wrong, if your mom's in the next room, if the fucking house is on fire..."

"Kind of." Tim's thinking of Ricky doing this to him. It would have to happen like this, because he couldn't ask for it.

Ricky reads it right out. "Almost like you wouldn't be responsible for it. You know? If it means so much to you, you'll do anything for it. And I don't have to say a word. I can make you my slave just by givin' you good sex. Just because you know if I'm pissed, you don't get it anymore. That's power. And you're not even hurtin' anybody."

"In a way you are."

"Maybe. You're just thinking of it from the wrong viewpoint. You're thinking of it from someone else's standpoint, not yours. You're too worried about what someone else will think."

"It matters. In cases like this."

"Tim, I'm just messing with your head, that's all."

Tim's a mess, all right. He's so consumed with Ricky's leathery presence, he can't think straight. There's so much hot body to look at, he doesn't know where to focus. Even the fingers. *Damn, look at it. Look what they could do!*

But Ricky's a little over being the belle of the ball, and he pops into the restroom to change back into the shirt and shorts. Has enough bags...looks like he spent the day at Marshall Fields. No one knows what lurks behind the man with the sexist message on his chest. Some girl walks up to him and says "I'm a virgin," and he says, "You deserve to be." No one has a sense of humor anymore.

Well, Sonia hates it, too. She won't let him wear it at home.

Back to the airport. *Gee, that was fun.* So bizarre. Just fly out, fly back. Rent a car, spend hundreds of dollars, back home, and presto!

Presto?

"Damn right," Ricky says. "P-R-E-S-T-O. You know, like real fucking fast. We live in a *presto* society. Mozart was smart. He'd be in and out of a *presto* in three and a half minutes. Haydn did it in a minute fifty-five. We keep it going for years at a time. It sucks. That's why I want out of accounting. Music lets you slow down every now and then. Work is all *now, now, now.* You're so lucky, Tim. You don't even know it."

Back in Ricky's apartment. He plays something on the piano. "I've been working on it." Chopin. A nocturne. Not too hard. Opus 15, No. 3. Not too fast. Slower later on.

"It's really pretty." Tim doesn't know Chopin from Charpentier.

"Thanks. It's even prettier when you play it right." Looking at Tim, looking, looking, enough of this looking. Time to put the pedal to the metal. Time to really see if this is it or not. He's never really taken charge of a man before. Always let Castor do it. This is the real thing. Not just a buddy thing, a real thing. A real gay guy. A little feeling. Castor never seemed really gay.

Ricky tries to figure out how to approach it delicately. He knows he's got a horrible track record with Tim. Everybody expects the worst from Ricky. They were raised that way. He knows he should pick up a random man at a random bar, but Tim's here and Tim's now.

So Ricky hugs Tim as thanks for the piano compliment. Just doesn't let go. Begins to kiss his ear, drag his tongue sloppily down Tim's neck. *Yeah, I can!*

Tim's afraid. So many feelings. It's so good, so right, so wrong. *Well, maybe he'll let go of me, and I can stop him.* Not until he lets go. At least take a little. Just a taste.

But Ricky won't quit. He can't lose the guts. Took him all day to get up the guts. Getting the rest up takes just a few seconds. Takes off his shirt, grabs Tim's and off it goes. Real fast. "Come on." Leads Tim into the bedroom.

"What are you doing?" Tim's a little mad, a little curious.

"Just what you want. I could see it."

"We can't do this."

"Stop me."

"Ricky, you're married. And I am. Castor's my lover. Not you."

Ricky cringes at the word *lover.* "He don't care."

"Yeah, he does." Tim protests, but he wonders.

"No, he doesn't. You're the one that cares. He'd worry more about me messin' with you than you messin with me."

"I know you've been with him."

"Yeah, I have. Been a long time. But Timmee, we got something. Something between us. You look me in the eye and tell me you don't want me to touch you—come on."

It's the damn power game. Tim's losing.

"Yeah, tell me I ain't good lookin' enough for you." He waits, and Tim's quiet. "I don't hear anything."

Tim's brain is so fucked up. Here's the dream of a lifetime, Ricky, the fantasy man...always the fantasy man. Here he is tearing me apart, and I can't have it.

A bit of a struggle for propriety's sake.

"How can you do this to your wife?"

"She won't let me do it to her."

"She's my friend!"

"Tim!"

Don't ask for it, you might get it—or something like that. The old Oscar Wilde tragedy of getting what you want. Far worse than not getting it. He kind of tries to push Ricky away. Ricky's too strong. All that working out, and he's got enough muscle to make Tim see things his way. *Good. I hoped he'd do this.* Overpowering. Look at him. *Look at his fucking body! Damn!*

"Come on, Timmee. You can touch me. I'm not made of glass. I've seen the way you're lookin' at me. All through the trip. I look at you the same way. I get tired of being the only hot man around. You're kinda hot yourself. A different kind of hot, but hot."

Ricky outweighs Tim by about fifty pounds, and it's all muscle. Tim's just got weight. Ricky pounces on top of Tim, pinning him down. Tim's in his greatest glory.

A kiss, a kiss, and yet another kiss. *Un baccio ancora,* Ricky thinks. Ricky just drools, a fountain of spit and tongue pouring into Tim's mouth. He's held back too damn long. Tongue winds down Dawson Road, over his lips, his nipples, his stomach. Tim can't stop him. Victory.

Thoughts of Castor, thoughts of Sonia. They're not here. Oh, Castor, I hope you'll understand. You've done it. You might still be doing it. A double immorality. He finally gives up, lets himself feel it how he wants to feel it. Tomorrow may never come.

Ricky's kind of rough. Not like Tim's used to. "You did it, Timmee, you turned me into the leather guy." It's so neat. Ricky's got the power. He can do it. It's not so bad. He can get anybody he wants and look who he wants. Got Sonia where he wants her. And Castor, who knows about Castor? Castor's fucking guys in Arkansas three days out of the week.

This doesn't count, anyway. It's not part of life. The whole day isn't part of life. Just do this, just to see if it's part of me. Then everything clicks back to reality. I better take what I can, because I can't keep it.

No turning back for Tim. Ricky's got him under a spell. All his body's just dying for Ricky, dying for his fingers, his lips, his strong rough arms moving him around like a pawn on a chessboard. *Wanna cum for him. Wanna show him how turned on he's got me. Against my will. I didn't ask. It's the only excuse I have.*

Tim loses it altogether. Yelps, gasps, twists, shouts, shoots, *God, it's hot, God, it's Ricky.* How can it be? Keep it low key, just keep it hot. The morality isn't so bad that way. Brings Ricky up to a pitch, hands moving over him, "Wanna see you cum, Ricky, want to real bad."

Yeah, I know. "Come on, guy, you can..." White shower glistens over dark hair, falling, falling, Tim looks down at his magic hands, the instruments of the perfect pleasure, Ricky's perfect pleasure, one and the same, Ricky flops around, smiles, gasps, over all too soon.

Tim feels like garbage. Betrayal, betrayal. Instant betrayal. The mind game is over. Ricky wins big time.

"Thank you!" Ricky's eternally grateful. Years of wondering finally paid off. It can work.

"Oh, RickyRicky." Says it again. "RickyRicky."

"TimmeeTimmee?"

"God we fucked up."

"Well, you're half right."

"Castor'd shit."

"No one will know unless your mouth starts spreading the cheese. Ain't it okay to do something for yourself once in awhile? I've been thinking for years. Always thinking of everyone else, and I wanted once in my life to do something for myself. And it's gonna be okay. We've been safe. Safer then I've been with Castor. He don't give a shit."

"He told me he..."

"Yeah. This is the first time I had a guy and I was sober. I needed to see if I could do it. If I could touch a man without being led into it. I knew I couldn't let you up. I couldn't lose my nerve."

"Well, it was good. Felt real good. And I do like you a lot. But we got too much to lose."

"I know. Sometimes you got to lose to win."

A couple showers, wash it all off. Blow dry, clean up the evidence. Change the sheets. Ricky changed them last Wednesday as well. Wants to show Sonia he can do some housework. She'll never notice. And she won't get laid tonight. Accounting never puts you in the mood to get laid. Music does.

"This is too bad in a way," Ricky says, and he sounds serious. Tim can never tell with Ricky. You have to read him real careful to see what he really means. What he says and what he means are so disparate, you have to think about everything that comes out of his mouth. "You and I have something together. You'll never have it with Castor, and I'll never have it with Sonia. But that's the way it is. And I'm too straight. You think I'm not, but I am. I know it. I know it." Ricky can't explain it. Some guys get a hankering for guys. Just every now and then. Hard to explain to a gay guy. He's never had to before. "It's just a shame it can't ever happen again."

The real thing. Tim can feel it. Ricky has a heart. And it's screwed up. Maybe he's not such a jerk after all. He's just on the wrong side of life. Not the straight thing. Just from every which way, on the wrong side. *Actually, we're both jerks.*

"See, you don't understand. Tomorrow, I go back to work. It's over. You're free still. I don't know how to leave the job. Today was like running away. I wish I could do it all the time. I wish so much, Tim."

"I'm sorry." Tim's near tears. He can feel it. "Castor's my running away. That's why if he ever found out about this here—"

"He won't find out."

"If I ever lose him, I don't know what I'll do. And I don't even know if I have him. I feel like I'm hanging on a cliff."

"Well, Tim, I will always be your friend. I can't speak for anyone else. Like I said, you and me have something. We need to stick together."

Tim remembers back to yesterday, when life was simple. Thinks a little more. "Hey, I forgot." How could he forget? Jeez! "I got your song." Pulls the cassette out of his pocket. "I forgot. Got so caught up in you I forgot about *us*." Pulls the words out of his wallet. Ricky's paper. It's been irritating him. Too much paper in the wallet. "Here."

Sitting on the couch, Ricky's arm around Tim's shoulders, following the lyrics over the coffee table, Tim's song on the stereo. It always sounds better on someone else's stereo. *Maybe we do have something together.* No one's heard this song yet. Dale's heard part of it. Tim's never used anyone else's words. It's so different. Kind of a funky feeling of lost love, rather than a driving feeling of frustration. A spartan bass, a stringy heavy treble. Emphasis more on the vocal. It works.

"We did it!" Ricky says.

Phone rings. *I'm going out for a bite to eat with the girls from class. I'll be home in about an hour.* An hour left. Life starts over.

"I had a great time, Tim. I'll let you know how the party turns out."

"I had a great time, too. You're okay, Ricky."

"Yeah? Thanks. You and Castor. Only friends I got. You wouldn't think it, but sometimes I feel like the loneliest man on the face of the earth. So, thanks for putting up with me." Ricky kisses Tim. His forehead, his nose, his lips, leaves a footprint in the sand. "We probably won't do it again."

"Do what?"

"Right." Tim steps outside. Comes back. Smiles. "You gotta take me home. You brought me here."

Ricky laughs, too. He needs it. Drive out silently, air conditioner on high. It's cool, but the AC brings life back into them. Tim understands. Tim tries to put it all away. Far, far back. He's going out with Sonia on Saturday. Staying over Castor's place Friday. Maybe Sunday. Why would Castor care more about Ricky? The unanswered question. Forget it. Ricky speaks too much truth to get his way. Tim's mind is a mess. It hurts, it hurts. But maybe Ricky's right. Just once, stop thinking about the rest of the world. Think of yourself. For once, goddammit, allow yourself to be happy. No, let's not.

But yeah, Castor won't know. I still love Castor. That'll never change. I can't love Ricky, anyway. I can love Castor. Now that it's happened once, this never has to happen again. I can love Castor forever.

Tim walks up the steps, past Dale's door. Is Darnell in there, happy and all that? Usually he'd knock, but not now. He spends all night staring into the lights of his stereo like an astronomer studying the galaxy. Thinking. He doesn't have to try. His mind works for him. Working overtime. *My heart is working overtime.*

My heart is working overtime.

Maybe something will come out of it.

Ricky comes home to a still empty house. Tired. Can't believe he spent all day on a plane. In a shop. In sober gay sex. Good time. Wait'll Sonia sees the costume! She'll love it. She'll die. The fairy godmother and the leather man. She looks stunning in hers. He thinks for a bit. With sequins, wings, red slippers...GLINDA...Sonia, Sonia, Sonia, *years back you'd never be late. Not if I was home.*

I wonder if you love me as much as I think I still love you?

Sonia comes in and puts on a light. Sees the paper on the coffee table. Scratch outs, lyrics, red pen? Some new piece of shit.

I wonder if you love me as much as I think I still love you?

Must be some other woman. He doesn't feel that way about me.

CHAPTER 9

Ricky comes jangling out of his room Friday night, walks into the living room. "Hey baby, wanna fuck?"

God, is he starting that shit again? Sonia turns around, wings brushing against the couch. Gasp-ola! "Where did you get that from?"

"Tim and I went up to Chicago Wednesday."

Sonia's used to a bit of leather because she's been to Mag's. On Ricky? Wow! "You went to Chicago with Tim?"

"Yep. Took him up, took him back. He picked it all out." Ricky gets it all out without even a revealing twitch. "Check the Visa bill next month if you don't believe me." She looks at him like he's crazy. "Just thought I'd surprise you."

"It's devastating!"

Thanks." It's been awhile since she's complimented him. "Let's knock 'em dead."

Which they proceed to do. The leather man and the fairy godmother. They get an unbelievable amount of attention. Both men and women are in awe of the whole thing. Odd, because Ricky doesn't really have a costume. It's nothing you have to make, just something you have to buy. But not for the Ladue crowd. Leather guys are "someone else" for these people. One of *them*. One of the deviants. Not someone you'd know.

Ricky and Sonia win the first prize for the best costumed couple, and Ricky gets his five hundred dollars and makes good on his promise to donate it back to the Shriners. Why have a party for the rich when your cause can use the money?

Standing up on the platform, him and his wife, everyone applauding. About two hundred people. He's afraid of the *Carrie* syndrome. Afraid that somehow a bucket of pig's blood is going to drop on his head. Maybe only symbolically, but he's not sure.

"No," the boss says, "You keep it. You've earned it."

No sense in arguing. *I'll get rid of it later.*

Yeah, the star shined. Ricky and Sonia get their pictures taken to get printed in the *Ladue News*. Great paper, if you like advertising and socializing. But the evening clicked. It's almost like they're married again. They're a couple. In everyone else's eyes, and even their own. *My Ricky. Mine. That gorgeous man in the leather outfit is* MY HUSBAND.

Sonia's got to take her wings off so she can get in the car. God, she's happy. Talky, bubbly Ricky remembers, vaguely, why he married her to begin with. *Did you see* him? *Did you see* her?

Damn, shut up already!

They get home, and he sits her down on the bed. She looks at him. So different. Almost a different person. It's the leather. If he'd have known, he'd have done this a year ago.

"Well, since I'm the fairy godmother, I can grant you three wishes," Sonia says, crossing her legs like a little coquette.

No problem with that. "To kiss you, to strip you, and to make luuuuuv to you."

She thinks for a little. "You'd do that to your godmother?" she smiles with a twinkle in her eye. Wow, her eyes are so beautiful. "Wishes granted!"

"Damn right it's granted," Ricky says. He smiles. *Maybe it's working. Maybe, maybe, maybe.* This is what he married her for. To have fun. So many people forget to have fun. *Fuckin' costume was worth every penny.* Gets closer to her. There's something so rude about taking the clothes off a fairy godmother. Something almost sinful as slowly he unbuttons, runs his fingers over the sequins. *Growl.* So be it. He's a leather guy. Even the fairies can't resist. Almost an escape here for him. Even his wife forgets about what a jerk he is. Finally. Orgasm without the baggage. Like Castor. Like Tim. Maybe like Sonia.

Ricky kicks his chains along the floor, pulling along a trail of broken hearts. Life goes on. *Life's a bleach and then you dye.* "You like your leather guy, don't ya'?"

"Yeah."

"I love you, Sonia. Never stopped..."

"I love you, Ricky." For once, she can let herself be taken by him. Just for once. Remember how it was? Remember, *it's so good because it's Ricky.* Let yourself go. It can be more than an obligation. It can be fun. Even with handsome hairy perfect body Ricky.

Next morning, Ricky wakes up and puts on faded jeans and a white t-shirt. Tonight's a Castor night. Sonia's afraid of Castor. She's hardly spoken to him in so long. Just at the parties, just politely. She's afraid mostly of Ricky *and* Castor. Castor himself isn't much of a hitch. But what's up with those two? Real life comes back to her, and it hurts more now.

Ricky looks like...Ricky. He's beautiful, but he's Ricky. Bouncing around the house, playing that damned Chopin nocturne, bouncing again. She's heard it so many times she could vomit. Why's he so happy? *Damn, it came right back.*

"Man, that was fun last night," he says.

"Great party."

"That's not what I meant."

"Oh, please, is that all it is to you?" Some women would do anything to have him all night, every night. She knows it. His fidelity is quite a plus in his favor. It must not be easy for him. Too bad she can't take advantage of it.

Ricky takes the second shot. She might as well have kneed him in the balls. He blows it up from a topical discussion to a tropical storm. He's had it. "What the fuck do you want out of me, honey?"

"What do you mean?" She doesn't say it kindly, either.

"I mean I love you till the fucking cows come home, and everything I do is wrong, wrong, wrong. I just thought it might be nice if we could be happy together. That's why I married you."

"I don't know." *Fuck you, too.* "It's just gone on for so long. Ricky, you just gotta grow up. You're such a kid." She's got a nasty sneer on her face.

"Grow up?" Ricky looks terrified. "I grew up a long time ago. Every time I touch the piano you act like I have to grow up. You know, if I could, I'd play it eight hours a day. Tim does."

"Tim doesn't have a job."

"I got money."

"Not enough to live on."

"We can move. We can get a Dogtown dive like you came from."

"Sometimes in life, you have to do things you don't want to do. I just wish you'd take on some responsibilities around here."

"Yeah, I guess you do." Saunters around a little, ducks down, eyes wide. "I guess one of yours is putting out for me. Sure ain't a pleasure. What happened last night? You forget who I was?"

"You always bring up sex. There's so much more involved. Can't you talk about anything else?"

"No. Not when you're not getting it."

She picks his song lyrics up off the coffee table. Sometimes Ricky feels his whole existence is embodied in that coffee table. "Then what's this all about?"

"Give me that!" Snatches them out of her hand.

"Who are they *for*?"

"What do you *care*?" Matches her note for note.

"Ricky, is there another woman?"

"No." He chooses his words carefully. "There is not another woman. And there oughta be."

"So I'm supposed to believe you."

He comes flying at her from across the room and grabs her roughly. "I've built my whole fucking life around you. Every damn thing I do for myself you don't like. Okay, all love aside—love's easy, honey, real easy—do you fucking *like* me at all?"

She looks at him. Holding her too close. Threatening. Afraid he might hit her. He never has. But it's a good question. And he's such a jerk. "I don't really know." *Gosh, it was so easy to say, too.*

"Cause I can send your ass back to Bleeck Street in a moment's notice."

"It's Bleeck Avenue, and I'm not going."

"It's up to you. I'm in this for keeps, but if you don't want it, I got self-esteem. I will not fold up and die, and I'd probably be a lot better off. And no fucking alimony, either. It's morganatic city for you, sweetheart." He pushes her away, walks off, and pounds the wall. She sits on the couch, waiting for the ocean to go back to sea.

Quiet. So quiet. Maybe she's gone too far. She looks at him, contemplates for a moment. Real quick, now—how would it be to wake up without him? Never to see him again? Go back out on her own. "You're right," she says. She takes his hand, looks in his eyes. Wants to say something nice to him, but can't think of what. He's got a stone expression but he's hurt deep. Four eyes with tears at the ready. "I'm gonna go for a while. I guess you'll be back tomorrow morning?"

Nod. It hurts so bad, the truth comes out like lava after so long.

"I'll see you then. Maybe we can start this mess over again." Flings her purse over her shoulder, out the door.

Ricky looks around. Tim's song crumpled on the floor. The tape's still there...

I wonder if you love me...

No need to wonder any more.

Ricky shows up at Castor's place about nine o'clock, leather outfit back in place. The hat, the harness, the full regalia. Castor's wearing his New Rutledge Outfit. Tim Dawson Outfitters, Inc., at work here.

Ricky runs a finger down Castor's nose. Castor's about out of control. "Wanna go to Clementine's...stud."

"Yeah!" Castor smiles. Looks like he's winning. Looks like Ricky's converted. "Yeah, I'll take ya." Castor hasn't been there in years. Hasn't been anywhere in years. At least nowhere in St. Louis.

For Ricky, it's the final hurrah. Going to a gay bar as a gay man.

Maybe the last time, who knows? Probably not, but it's a pretty deep dive for him. Tomorrow, Sonia says she's gonna make it work. We'll see. Tonight we play.

"Ricky, you look wicked! Unbelievable."

Not a far journey from Castor's place. I-44 to 18th Street, down Lafayette, down 9th Street, down Allen, there we go. Castor's surprised he remembers. The Soulard neighborhood where all this is located has changed a lot, it seems. Spotty rehabbed place. Some blocks are trendy, some are falling apart, some are plain fucking wealthy. The door to Clementine's is the pathway to broken hearts and country music. The two seem to go together. Guys standing around by the jukebox, the phone, the pool table. The bar in the middle of the place, dark walls around it, red lights, black and white checkered tile floor.

Guys stand agape at the entrance of the two Dawson Outfitters clients. Nobody's seen them before. Whispers, stares, smiles. It happens. It's real. They're *hot*. Especially that dark haired guy! No, I like the other one. Kinda has that rough look to him.

Ricky's never seen it before. He doesn't know what to do. Talk to someone? Everyone wants to. Get a drink? Of course. What else? Go to the bar and ask for a beer like it's nothing. Like you're the guy in the TV ad. "I'll have a beer," he says.

Bartender looks at him funny.

"Bud Light. Sorry."

"Oh, don't be sorry. You new in town?"

"Yeah." Ricky means it symbolically.

"Where you from?"

"Creve Coeur."

"How come we ain't never seen you in here before?"

"Cause you ain't never been lucky," Ricky says. He's confident. It's amazing. All these people tired of the same faces. The same men with overhanging bellies, tired eyes, and bad attitudes trying to look like studs. Here's the real thing.

Lots of handshakes as Ricky and Castor introduce themselves. Ricky looking the crowd over. Anybody from work? Just wondering. Anybody I'd like to meet? Just wondering.

Guy comes up to him. "Is he your lover?"

Ricky looks over to Castor. "Yep." Has no choice, apparently. String attached to this trip. Castor said it in the car. "If anybody asks, tell them you're with me. They won't bug you." *Maybe I want them to. Maybe I should have come by myself.*

Guys start bugging him. Out on the back patio, Castor and Ricky are standing around. Some shorter kind of effeminate guy comes up to Ricky and rubs the top of his chest, tangles his fingers in the hair. "Ohh, that's really nice. I know I'm not your type, but I like this."

Ricky's not used to it, being groped in public.

An older guy comes by. Kind of bigger. "Where you come from?"

"Little Rock. Me and Castor trucked up for the weekend."

"You're hot."

"Ricky."

"Dennis."

"Hey, Dennis."

Castor's a couple feet behind, watching. Dennis is up to something. Got a hand on Ricky's face. Pulling at his mustache, at his shoulders, messing with the hair on his chest. A real hair freak, and Ricky's too uncovered. Dennis moves the vest aside, starts playing with a nipple. Ricky feels odd, being out here where everyone can see. "You and me could probably find somewhere to go," says Dennis. "I could lick you from head to toe and then some."

Castor goes over and pulls Dennis's arm away. Holds his wrist real tight. Castor's got a vice grip from the steering wheel. "If I were you, I'd go take my lickin' to somebody else."

"I think Ricky can make up his own mind." Looking for trouble.

"See, yeah, but Ricky don't tell you everything." Castor's deadpanning again. "See, last time Ricky went home with somebody, I got a little upset, and I took it out on Ricky's friend. They had to put me away for two years."

Dennis knows people. He wants to get Castor kicked out, but then Ricky has to leave as well. Tough titties, as they say.

Finally some people to talk to. Just to talk. Ricky knows it's cause of what he looks like. Conversation gets weird on him. *Have you ever done this? Have you ever done that? I had a guy once who...*

No, but I play a little Chopin.

I'm a church organist. You should come tomorrow morning.

Everyone seems to be a church organist. Ricky wonders if the priests don't just come to Clementine's to find them.

Castor makes the best of his one night lover status. He holds Ricky's hand. He rubs Ricky's shoulders. Every now and then a kiss. Once a big long one. Tongue under the lip. Castor gets Ricky's mustache up under his as the mustache freaks watch the black and blond hair tangle up on their top lips. Feels good. Ricky doesn't mind. No one comments on the ring. Starlight shines on the patio, gleams off the ring. Look around, they've put out pots of flowers. Petunias, ferns, all kind of things.

This isn't half bad, Castor thinks. *It's quiet out here. We can talk. And I'm with my man.* He's not really in awe of the countless men around him. Ricky kind of is. It's his first immersion into homosexual society. All the costumes. The leather, the impersonators, the guys, just normal guys out for a drink. More than one wants him to come home. Some want him and Castor. Who's to say? Nobody seems to be better look-ing. Envy, envy, envy. *Well dammit, if you'd work out two hours a day you could look like this.*

No honey, I could work out every hour of my life and I'd never come close.

Thanks.

Twelve fifteen, twelve thirty. Ricky's only had a couple. Castor's only had a couple. He wonders what's up. Never seen it before. He's afraid to ask. Afraid that it might all vanish if he questions it. They've never really talked about it, just did it. Now, maybe it's Ricky's way of showing Castor that he's ready.

"Where'd you get all that leather from anyway?"

"Me and Sonia went to a costume party. Tim kinda picked it for me."

Don't mention her name. "Yeah. Tim would know what to do." A few beats. "Musta done it while I was gone."

"Wednesday. Flew up to Chicago and back. Just a whim."

"It looks good. I know a million people have said this, but you are a good looking guy."

"You too, Castor."

"Nah."

"Yeah. I'm goin' home with ya'. You too, Castor."

"Yeah." Smiles.

One thirty comes down, guys want Ricky to go to Magnolia's.

How long you gonna be in town?

Just tonight. Gotta truck back tomorrow.

Then you gotta go to Mag's.

Sonia's at Mag's. So near, and yet so far.

Castor's gettin' horny. He don't like to be kept waitin'.

127

Parole officer, you know. He don't let me stay in Missouri any longer than I need to.

Ricky's got to kiss about five guys goodbye. Some of them have developed quite an emotional attachment to him, but none as much as Castor. Back in the Ford, Ricky busts out laughing. "Man, you've got the sickest sense of humor. Two years."

"Got it from you."

"But Castor..."

"What?"

"I wanted that guy."

"He don't want you. He just wants one thing." Castor's up, happy, hasn't felt this way in ages.

"Yeah, Mom."

"And you know what?"

"What?"

"I want the same thing."

"Well, then let's go out with a bang." Ricky looks down at his ring. "I'm surprised they didn't notice this."

"They did. I said I bought it for you."

"Oh, man," Ricky says. "We were a *serious* couple. They'll never know we're both happily married men."

"I didn't wanna watch them pawing at you." Castor's high as a kite, as they say. Wide awake, happy as can be, all the clichés. Ricky isn't drunk. He's all together and seems to be agreeable. Seems to be going Castor's way.

Another kiss in the driveway. He moans deep into Ricky's mouth. Castor never was much into kissing before. It's a love thing for him.

He gets Ricky inside. Into his room. Closes the door. Music still plays in his head, some of that disco stuff he remembers a little from ten years ago. Some new stuff, just the beat goes through his head. A little more attuned to it because of Tim. Eyes clear over the room, they see a pile of Tim's tapes on the stereo. Tim's clothes in the closet, on the floor. *We'll have to see about that, won't we?*

Castor on the edge of the bed, looking at a standing Ricky. Eye view of his bare stomach. Tongue reaches out, touches. "You know, one thing about leather guys," Castor explains. "They get to do whatever they want." Takes Ricky's hand, each finger into his mouth, all the way down. Takes his time. This is amazing, this is real, this tastes like a man. Ricky's got the rings. The engagement ring, the wedding ring, another ring of turquoise just for effect. Fingers are better. Just bare fingers. Castor works his teeth around the rings, pulls them off slowly.

Ricky feels the sensation—teeth, tongue, lip, lets it happen. It's his last night. Maybe. Sees the diamond ring looped on the edge of Castor's tongue. Castor spits it across the room; it falls down into the no-man's land behind the dresser. Oh, well. Ricky knows he's going to get the performance of his life. *Allegro, Adagio, Menuetto,* and *Finale: Presto.* His wife just said she didn't like him. Tomorrow they start over. How, after six years, do you wipe a slate clean? *Maybe like this. Maybe just for me.*

This makes three people in four days for Ricky. He's never done that before. He wasn't raised that way. Kind of rebellious for him. They've all betrayed each other on his account. Sex as power. *Power, power, power—why am I such a slave to you, Castor?* Castor's got him on such a roll, and he can feel the absence of the ring. Down in the bottom of the Rhine. Without the Rhinemaidens, even. He can feel his hand, so free, just a taste of freedom. Some obscure Haydn minuet goes through his mind. Can't even place it. Just went there.

The whole world centers on Ricky Rutledge, funneled through Castor. Finally...climax, collapse. Castor takes a handful of cum and wipes it down Ricky's face. There isn't that much, gotta use it carefully. Ricky lets him. Hard hands oiling him up. Let go, let go, *I'm a leather guy, I'm into this.* It's going to be a mess to clean up.

Finally Castor cuddles up to Ricky, arm around him. Close to him, warm, Ricky's ready to drift off to sleep. So many times he's done it with Castor's arm around him. It's easy. It's the only arm he's had around him in a long time. Ricky can smell the sweat and the scent. It's something, at least.

"Ricky?" Voice breaks through the sleep barrier.

"Mmmm."

"Ricky..."

"Yeah."

Castor steels himself for the task at hand. "I love you, Ricky."

"Mm. Yeah." Pause, sleep...no, no, what did he say? Eyes bang open, staring at the wall. Train goes by. Jazz chord. Sounds like the Manhattan Transfer. Quiet, and a few crickets. Castor's asleep with his Ricky held tight. Breath hits the back of his neck. He wonders if maybe he's played the game a little too long. A little too successfully now that he's Don Juanned through the world of gay men. A world suddenly so alien, he longs for home.

CHAPTER 10

"You have to accept people the way they are. You can't change them. It's either take it or leave it," Tim says to Sonia. "But I can't do it either."

Tim and Sonia are at the Missouri Botanical Gardens. She showed up at his door about seven hours early but to Tim, that's more an expression of friendship than a major irritation. The Garden seemed like a nice place to go. Maybe.

"It looks like my mother-in-law's house," Sonia frumps upon arrival.

Of course, most of the afternoon is taken up by a discussion of their errant spouses. Sonia can hardly talk about it because this time it's her fault, *but Ricky made me this way. And you, Tim. I know Castor's my brother, but you need to find someone better than him. Someone who'll treat you right.*

Walking through rows and rows of fauna. Flowers, hostas, trees, the Japanese Garden where they're on a small bridge looking down at koi in the fish pond. Not a bad day. A little hot, but breezy.

"Can't give him up," Tim says. "He's all I got. And I'm tired of everyone telling me to give him up."

"Yeah, I guess that could get old. My mother never liked Ricky. She kept telling me not to marry him. Now I hardly speak to her. Funny thing is, she was right to begin with. But we're gonna try it. We're gonna try to make it work out, but I don't know. If he won't change, then it's all up to me. And I don't know if I can stand him."

Tim's real touchy on the Ricky subject. He thinks Ricky's right and Sonia's wrong, but he doesn't want to blow the friendship. Just let her talk. Don't repeat anything.

He's not doing bad here in being a best friend to the woman he recently betrayed. It's so far from her mind. She wouldn't think of it. Tim tries not to, but if he's not thinking about it, he realizes he's not thinking about it and starts again. So sometimes he gets a little lost, and Sonia has to phase him back to reality. *I just get that way sometimes. Just a little depressed, that's all.*

Yeah, Ricky was so good to him. But it was a one time thing. Seems strange that a friend can be so perfect to you and then say it can't work, so goodbye. Not really goodbye, but this is all it is. Well, that's life. At least there's the thought. Maybe it will happen again. Looking at Sonia, thinking of the night with her husband. Ricky's hands, Ricky's face, Ricky's cock. The Dawson morality doesn't wash with it, so he's got to rearrange a lot of brain cells to put things on different shelves. One thing has nothing to do with the other.

"Something's going on with Ricky," Sonia says. "I just don't know what."

"Maybe it's something good."

"It hasn't been yet."

After the garden, it's dinner and hanging out at Tim's place, and Magnolia's about nine o'clock. Finally. Everyone's happy to see Sonia. She should come out more often. Well, she can't. But it's good to be here.

Saturday's a fun night. Everybody's everywhere, going from bar to bar. Some guys walk in about eleven or so. *Damn Tim, there was this guy at Clem's, and he was so fucking hot. Hairier than shit! Couple of truckers from Little Rock. God, I just about jacked off on the way over here.*

Tim is paralyzed with fear, but he can't let on. *Will you shut up?* He wants to scream it.

Maybe some guys from out of town, they say.

Get away from these guys, and forget, fast. "Let's dance, Sonia. Okay?"

"Sure!" Sonia's dressed down from the first time she came here. The dress is gone. Just jeans and a shirt. She looks a little cowboy. Put a hat on her and it's Janie Frickie in a minute.

She's got a lot of energy, a lot of frustration pent up. All night long in the back of her head, Ricky's standing there reacting to her last statement. She wonders if tomorrow will be any better. Sometimes when you walk out the door setting everything on fire along the way, you say things out of context just for effect. *Start over? With what?* It's like playing Monopoly with no money. You keep going because you were having a good time once.

Suddenly the music stops and the dance floor goes quiet. An altered voice comes over the loudspeakers, in that mock seriousness that dance music made famous.

> *Even though you've made me cry*
> *My love for you will never...die.*

Drumbeats start up on *die*. Slower, deliberate, loud, funky. Dawson. Tim gave the song to Chuck Thursday. Getting better and better. *Yeah, Tim, you're goin' somewhere!*

It's all oddly familiar. The words come through to Sonia in a scrawled out version of Ricky Rutledge. In red. Familiar...

Longing for the days when my heart beat just for you
I wonder if you love me as much...as I think I still love you

"Tim, where did you get those words?"

"Ricky wrote it."

"I know. I saw it."

"He wanted to surprise you."

"Is it for me?"

"Yes it's for you. You're the only woman in his life."

"Well," She puts out her hands like she gives up. "I'm surprised."

"It was the best way he could say he cares about you."

"I don't know what to say." *Maybe he does love her. He's still a jerk, but it hurts her now, too. Maybe she could have given in a little more.*

"Ricky's a special kind of guy," Tim tells her. "He just needs a lot of understanding." *Which I have, and you don't.*

"I guess so. Well, let's dance to it. It's a great song, Tim. No matter who wrote the words."

Another success. The TimRicky songwriting machine. *Maybe Ricky can get better, save me a little trouble writing.* He's coming from the same place. Frustrated love.

Sonia's mind is a little screwed up now. She deserves it. She started it. Every night for a few months now, it's going to go out to the whole dancing gay world, at least the only dancing gay world she knows of. Her song. Wonderful. Having her whole wasted life blasting out at a volume louder than a fucking jet plane. Wonderful.

Three o'clock or later, maybe, she gets home again. Afraid of tomorrow, afraid of tonight, just afraid.

Ricky's up early the next morning. Can't get much sleep. It wasn't supposed to be this way. Just buddies. What's this *I love you* shit?

Castor thinks he's got it made. It's only a matter of time. Ricky's got
to go home, but he'll be back.

Another long kiss goodbye. Ricky wonders whence cometh it from?
He must have learned it from Tim. Castor never was much on it before.
Still feels the same, but different in the mind. Now it means something.

Ricky gets in around eleven o'clock. Sonia's eating. Ricky sits down
across from her at the little table in the dining area. Says hi. She says hi.
He doesn't know what to do. Opens up a newspaper that Sonia's picked
up. Sunday. Lots of stuff going on. All she can see are his hands and the
top of his head. Looking, looking, *what is it?*

"Where's your ring?"

"What do you mean?"

"I mean, your rings are missing."

"Oh. Yeah. Castor's got 'em."

"What is Castor doing with your rings?"

Impish. "I'll never tell."

"Ricky..."

Shit, here we go again. He looks at the clock and mumbles. "Hmm,
five minutes... five minutes of peace before we start this all over again."

"Ricky, those rings are worth five thousand dollars. At least. He'll probably sell them before you see him again. What did you take them off for?"

He smiles, almost evil. "Hee hee hee. You'll never know."

"What's goin' on? There's something happening with you and Castor, and I want to know what it is."

Taunting all the way. Not the way to fix the marriage, but he can't seem to help himself. "I bet you do." Eyes wide, kind of slinking in his chair. Singsong voice. Paper comes down, Ricky looks at his fingers spread wide. Didn't even notice it. Too much on his mind.

"What are you doing with Castor?" She's rigid, glaring from across the table.

"Why are you making such an issue of this?"

"You made the issue of it. I asked you a question."

"And I told you'"

"Maybe I'm just wondering what you're doing that you need to take off your wedding ring on a Saturday night out."

Ricky has a choice here. He can either say, *It'd be nice if you gave me a fucking reason to wear it* or *Castor pulled it off.* Split second, what'll do the most damage? "Castor pulled it off." *We'll leave out the "with his teeth" part.*

"What for?" Now she's really curious.

"Just messing around. You know how guys get."

She does. She just went to Magnolia's. "I didn't realize men pulled off each other's wedding rings in the course of 'messing around.'"

"Me neither. You don't know Castor too well anymore, do ya'? He play rough." Hands out like doggy paws. "Ruff, ruff, ruff."

"You go back and collar him and get them back."

Oooohhh, authority! The look on his face speaks that one. "I'll get them when I get there."

"Ricky. Make me happy. Please. Go get 'em. This isn't a good time to throw around the symbols of our marriage."

"Or," he says, spitting on the table, "spit them out." Somehow the idea of thousands of dollars' worth of diamonds flying across the room strikes Ricky as pretty funny.

* * *

Castor's getting the third degree as well. Made the mistake of telling the truth.

"What'd you do last night?"

"Took Ricky to Clem's."

"Why'd you do that?"

"Because he wanted to go."

"You never take me."

"You never asked to go to Clem's."

"You wouldn't go anyway." Tim finds this impossible to deal with, taking Ricky to a gay bar. "I keep trying to get you to go to Magnolia's and you won't ever go."

"You're right."

"Just makes me feel like shit."

"Tim!" Castor's over this one already. "I didn't take him there to hurt you. He came to the door and asked me to take him. Even called me stud. Man, if Ricky called you stud you'd take him to the fuckin' moon, wouldn't you?"

"Yeah, don't get so high and mighty on Ricky!" *I've had him.*

"It's just something special I did for him."

"Why don't you do anything special for me?"

"Because you're here all the goddamn time!" Almost a scream. Castor exhales angrily. "And I don't want to spend all day in a fuckin' argument. You asked what I did, an' I told you. I could start lyin' to you if you'd rather. If you don't like it, you got your own place."

Well, that didn't work. "Sorry."

The phone rings.

"Hello." Castor's curt. Some mumbo jumbo on the other end. Castor smiles a bit. Demeanor changes. "Yeah, come on. Come on. Yeah, I got 'em. We'll fit 'em right back." Hangs up. "Well, Timmee, Ricky's comin' over. You gotta git."

"What for?"

"We got something to talk about."

"Well, I can hang out somewhere."

"Tim, please. It's kind of a private thing. You'll find out soon enough. I promise. No more secrets."

"You'll call me when he goes?"

"Maybe. See how it works out, what's up."

Tim's ready to cry. Just a bit. If he doesn't see Castor today, he won't see him again until Friday or whenever he gets back in town. It's so long. He's afraid of the pain during the wait. Every goddamned week of his life he's got to live with it. "I won't see you 'til Friday, then."

"Well, then I won't see you 'til Friday then, either. Works both ways."

Tim feels a little better. Wonders if Castor thinks of him on his trips to Arkansas. "I love you, Castor."

A hug. Tim clings on for dear life. "Yeah, Timmee. I know."

Hard to talk, for some reason. Some bad reason. Ricky ain't a good reason to leave. "I'll see you then." Barely above a whisper. "See you, Mrs. Williams." On the way out. *What does she know? Any ideas about all that's gone on in that little back room?*

Castor's smiling to himself, checking out the mirror, giving himself the thumbs up sign. Maybe Ricky's right. *You are a good looking guy.* Just a little scraggly's all. Smile won't go away. It's time.

Ricky walks past Emma without saying much. There isn't much to talk about. Into Castor's room. Castor greets him with a tight hug, a wet kiss, an unusual self-assurance as if everything is set for good. Big time. "She's such a bitch today," Ricky says. "I gotta get those rings and bring them right back. I don't know what her problem is with it."

"Yeah. She is a bit of a bitch, isn't she?" Castor lays back on the bed, arms behind his head, inviting. Confident. "You know Ricky, I don't think I'm *gonna* give 'em back to you."

"Castor. I need 'em. I'm in big fucking trouble."

"See..." Slowly, almost like a lawyer. "I think the time has come for you to make up your mind."

"About what?" Like he doesn't know.

"About me and her. I don't think you're gonna need the rings anymore. I think it's time for you to maybe stick here with me." Eyes up. Tempting for a moment?

"Castor, I can't do that."

He never thought of that. "Why not?"

"'Cause I'm straight, that's why."

"No ya' ain't."

"Yeah, I am."

Castor thinks for awhile. *How to do this?*

Ricky sits down on the bed. *How to do this?*

"Ricky... Come here, Ricky."

"Let me stay here." Scared shitless. Great name for a movie, anyway. *Scared Shitless.* A David O. Selznick Production.

"Okay. Ricky. Remember last night?"

"Yeah."

"I notice you. You're gettin' more and more into me. You're likin' me more, makin' me feel real good. You know me, I don't tell much of what I'm feelin', but I never felt this way about a man like I do about you. I think I could make it work with you. And I think you could make it work with me."

"I could," Ricky says.

"You know I'm the only one of all of 'em who treats you worth a shit. I'm the only one. Sonia don't care. Emma don't care. Ted and Betty don't care. I love you, Ricky."

"Yeah, I know you do. And I love you, Castor. But not in the same sense. You're my friend. Kind of a close friend."

"Real close."

"Yeah, real close. Close enough to suck your dick, huh? But my heart is with her. Or a woman. It's how I am. I don't think I could make an emotional commitment to a man, I guess. You know what I mean. Otherwise—"

"Otherwise? Man, you're awful emotional to me. You tell me everything, do everything. You do shit in bed some guys would puke at." His world is crumbling, continent by continent.

"Castor, when I'm thinkin' about sex, I think about women. You're the only man I've ever had." *So I lied a little. So sue me.* "It's my feeling for you. And maybe I'm a little bi or something. But I couldn't be your lover."

"Garbage, Ricky. You might think it. Guys think it a lot. They get scared of what the world thinks, and it makes them decide something that isn't true. Then they realize that they *do* want a man. Lots of 'em were married before."

"That's not the way it is." Ricky's got this set expression on his face. He can't get through. "Lots of guys have their wives and just like a little dick on the side."

"So, I'm a dick on the side?"

"No. I was just saying that."

Castor scoots up to the edge of the bed and puts his hands on Ricky's shoulders. Looks into that beautiful face, seeing a lifetime slipping away. "I could be a good man for you. I could be good to you." He hears himself pleading. Not like him, but he can't stop. He's got to win with this much at stake.

"I know you could." Ricky feels like shit as well. This wasn't supposed to happen. "I guess we never talked about this before. Maybe we should have. I was afraid to. But my mind is not oriented like yours. You might sleep with some gal a couple nights, but you wouldn't want anything else to do with her. Tim really cares for you. Stick with him. He's a good guy."

"I don't *want* Tim! Damn. I told you I loved you. I never said that before. Not even to Tim."

"Castor, I have to go. I can't stay here too long now. Can't we talk about this later?"

"Why. Goin' back to her? You like gettin' bitched at all day and all night? Never gettin' any? I treat you better than that. I never screamed at you in my life."

"I know. You're one of the few good things I have."

"It can be better." Holding Ricky's hand. Ricky's returning it. Castor looks at Ricky's face. His eyes are fluttering. His breath is heavy, lips are moving, twitching, grasping. "Look at you. Ricky, damn you're shaking."

"I don't want to do this to you, Castor. Don't make me do this."

"I can move out of here. Get a job in town, so you won't be lonely. We'll get along good."

"Castor, I can't do it. How many times—"

"Never be enough. I don't believe you. You're just saying it because you think you're so damn macho with all those chicks. I make you feel good. Don't I? Something I don't do right?"

"No. That's not it."

"Then what is it?"

"It's me, Castor. I want my goddamn marriage to work out. Okay? You might not think I'm straight. Cause you're the man I've had. The one man. It took me awhile to get into it."

"Don't matter how long." Castor's looking at the floor now. Feels lost. "God, I've never felt like this about anyone ever," he says. "I don't know if I could feel it again. It's hard for me. To love. But when I met you and got to know you, it got real easy to think about you, to hold you. To know you'd always be my friend."

"And I always will be."

"I know. But it's not...I need you."

"Castor, we'll..." There's not much else to say. "I don't know how to make it any better."

"You can stay with me."

This will go on forever. Ricky gets up. "I can't. I gotta go. Where's the—"

"Ricky, please!!" Look up into his eyes, his beautiful dark eyes. Watering. Pools of water. "You're cryin', man. You're cryin' for me and walkin' out."

I don't want to go home to her. That's all it is. "It hurts to watch."

"Maybe you need a little more time. To make up your mind."

"Sonia or no Sonia, I don't think I can be gay. Not for a lifetime. You don't see that, but that's the way I am."

Let it all go. It's your only chance. "Just know I love you. I don't know what'll happen if you go."

"I have to go."

Castor grabs Ricky, leans his head on Ricky's belt. *Just yesterday we were like this, so good, so perfect. And he liked it all.* "Please don't go. You're all I have. I'll be so alone."

"I'm sorry. If it's any consolation, I feel like a real shithead."

"Don't matter what you feel like if you're gonna walk away."

"Can't you see? I don't have a choice. If I could, I'd be with you in a minute."

"Right. You could."

Ricky hurts so much, but he can barely look at Castor. Calm, cool Castor, nearly at his feet like a wrecked truck. "Castor..." Whisper. "I have to go."

Castor nods, still looking down. Feels the lump welling up in his throat. Can't even say bye. Never cried before. No sound, just tears, silent mourners drop off his face onto Ricky's belt. Can't look up. Can't risk being seen. Can't let go. It's over if he does. Never the same. Lip trembles. Breath comes in gasps, when he can. He'll stay here all day if he has to. Strong grip will keep Ricky here. *Ricky won't really leave if I don't let him. He loves me. I know he loves me. Starve to death, if I have to. I'll hold you forever.* "I love you, Ricky." *May as well say it one more time. Maybe it will change his mind.*

"It's gonna be okay."

Castor bites his lip, shakes his head. *No. It won't.*

"I'll talk to you. Soon." Ricky gets loose and goes off. Lights out. Exit stage. Curtain. Castor sits on his bed, tears falling off his face like a slow spring rain. Doesn't even try to stop them.

Few minutes later, Emma comes to the doorway. It takes her a bit, but she's there. Never seen it before.

"Ricky didn't look too good. What happened?"

143

Castor doesn't have the strength to hide. "I love him. And he's gone. Mom, he's gone. Back to..."

"Castor, I never knew."

"She took him from me, Mom. He loves me. I know it. And he's the only man in the world that I can love."

Emma holds up a brown and yellow sweater. "I made this for you. I hope you like it."

Castor sees it. Smiles a bit through faster tears. "Thanks. I thought it was for the cat." Gives Mom a hug. It's been years. "I'll use it. I promise."

"I don't know why I never thought to make it for you before. Tim suggested it."

"Yeah. He's good that way."

"You and me oughta stick together. We're the only family we have." A look at each other, a long, lost feeling. "I don't know what to do. If there's anything—"

"She ain't keepin' him!" Hand cuts the air. Words are still a struggle. "You watch, she ain't keepin' him. I'll see to it."

"You look like you need to be alone."

Alone never felt so real.

CHAPTER 11

Door slams and two pictures crash to the floor. Sonia jolts up. Ricky's got the most distraught expression she's ever seen. She doesn't know what to say, if she should say anything at all.

"I hope you're fuckin' happy," he says.

"Did you get them back?"

"No." Hands spread in the air. "He wouldn't give them to me."

"*Damn* him!"

"Fuck *you!*"

Life is hell at the Rutledge place. Now they've got to wait until Castor gets back off the road. Since Ricky doesn't have a wedding ring, the whole female population is going to be under the mistaken impression Richard K. Rutledge is available for marital hire. Not to mention the guys at the gym. *Maybe she's right.* It is five thousand dollars' worth of jewelry collecting dust in Castor's bedroom. And any way you look at it, five thousand dollars is five thousand dollars.

Can't get them Monday. Never call Castor on Monday. It's just an unwritten rule. If he's here, Monday's his day to do stuff for mom. "God, he lets that woman run his life," Sonia complains.

"Well, what have *you* done for her in the last five years?"

* *
*

Tim paces the week like a tiger in a cage. He can't pounce. All he can do is wait for bad news. Unfortunately, it's really good news he hears. Dale comes to the door with more exciting things to say about his newfound relationship.

"He said he loves me!"

"He hardly knows you."

Dale is shocked but not surprised. "Tim, he said he loved me. Be happy."

"I am happy, Dale. For you." Everything Dale says drives home a truth that's about to reveal itself like a bad prize on *Let's Make a Deal*. Hard to be happy for someone who has what you so desperately want. It shouldn't be, but it is.

Dale can sense something. He finally simmers down and listens. And listens. An hour goes by, and Tim's talked a galaxy of circles around his problem.

"Guess we won't be double-dating anytime soon."

"Guess not."

Dale hugs Tim. Tim needs it. "Look, we've been friends forever. I don't know what I'd do without you. This guy, he ain't for you. You deserve better, and I don't think he really wants you. Sorry, Tim."

Tim goes to the window. "Why's everybody so down on this?"

"Because it's a downer. You tell me how miserable you are, and now you want me to tell you to stay with it? 'Hey Tim, you're riding a train off a cliff, stay on the train.' That's not my job. Sorry if it bugs you that I found someone. I won't bring it up anymore."

"That's not it." Tim still hasn't stopped pacing.

"Okay, then." Dale's dizzy from watching, so he grabs Tim's shoulders and holds him still. But he's serious, and he looks Tim deep in the eyes, which says so much more than his words. "If I can't talk about

Darnell, you can't talk about Castor."

Tim can't do that, so he's stuck listening to good things about Darnell. *Go away, Dale. Not now. Keep that smile downstairs. I shoulda been with you, and I'd have that same smile right now.*

Castor drives Tuesday, watching the road, in a groove, in a rut. The escape comes and goes. Sometimes a tear falls from his eye. Hard to believe. The one time in life he tried to join in, now even that's gone. Maybe he shouldn't have said anything. Ricky would have kept coming by. At least it was something. But Ricky wasn't going to say it. Castor had to. It was so hard, and he prepared for so long. What was the worst that could happen? Probably this. Gaze down the road, don't look around, just drive. Maybe keep driving.

Maybe. Maybe he could have said something to make Ricky understand. But after *I love you,* everything else falls flat.

Unload the truck in Little Rock, hang out at the truck stop. He goes in the restaurant with his trucker outfit of torn jeans and plaid shirt. Doesn't care what he looks like today. Trip to the men's room, glance in the mirror, hair's a mess. Yellow and lifeless, almost like his face. Look in the mirror. *No wonder he didn't want me. Look at this shit!*

Castor orders a burger and mashed potatoes. He's faced with the whole evening by himself. Usually no problem, but he can't stand it. No one to tell it to. Can't talk to Tim, can't talk to Ricky.

He gets an idea. Throws everything out of his wallet all over the table, receipts, money, I.D—there it is. Matthew Texas Barlotti. What the heck?

There's a phone at the table; some of the truck stops do this for an interesting convenience. He dials the number. Some dumb Arkansas hoosier picks it up looking for trouble.

"Yeah what?"

Here, they say redneck. In St. Louis, it's hoosier. Same thing.

"I said yeah, what you want?"

Yeah yourself. "Matt there?"

"I don't know where y'all come from, but around here we say hello first."

Fuck you. "Hello. Is Matthew there?"

"Who's this?"

"Castor."

"Ain't ya got a first name?"

"Bill Castor."

"What you want with Matthew? You a fag or something?"

Castor gets gruff, and he's already edgy. "I know where you live, and I know what your ugly ass looks like, and this is one tough faggot that'll break you in three bloody but equal pieces."

That worked. "Matth-yew!! You know a guy named Bill Castor?"

"Give me that! Dammit Trevor, give me the phone! Hello!"

"Hey, Matthew Tex."

"Hey, Castor Bill. *Trevor, get the fuck out of here!* Sorry, it's my brother. He's a fuckhead."

"No wonder you left. Well, look, Matth-yew. I'm in town tonight if you—"

"Yeah. I kept hoping you'd call."

"Well, I'm here. Things ain't too good. Um...I'm not doin' well, but I thought you could come meet me here at this truck stop."

"Yeah. What's up?"

"Lost my man. Just need someone..." All this soul baring. Really hard to do. No way out, though.

"I'll be right there." If there's one thing Tex knows, it's how to get to a truck stop.

"I'll be in my truck." He describes it so Matthew Tex can find him.

"And where do you think you're going?" Dad or someone, nasty in the background.

"I'm going out. Hey Castor Bill, I'll see you."

Matt's gotta fight his way out of the family cottage. They don't care what he's doing, but he might be enjoying himself somewhere and they've got to put a stop to it.

Castor finishes up his burger and his mashed. He has a little appetite to quell, but not much. Pays, goes to wait in the sleeping area in the back of his cab. Sees Matthew coming through the lot. Castor's on his small bed, mostly undressed. Matt climbs in, gives a quiet greeting, holds him silently for awhile. Usually this would be a sexual situation, but it all seems useless right now. Finally Matt sits up on the bed, takes Castor's hand.

"He gone?"

Castor nods. Doesn't need to say anything. Just needs a neutral party. "Sorry I called you like this. I ain't gonna be any good tonight."

"It's okay. I just wanted to see you again."

"You did?"

"Yeah. I like you. I think about you a lot. Things are crazy at home, if you hadn't noticed."

Small consolation. "Usually I just stay here and smoke and drink. Page through trucker magazines. Written for guys like me that don't read. Ain't much. But if you ain't too bored on me, you can stick around."

At least you ain't screamin' at me. "I'll stay. It's nice just holding your hand and being quiet." Castor looks around his little alcove: just

149

a couple things to wear and a place to sleep. Some guys really do it up, but not him. Sky darkens slowly outside. Silent man next to him. He thought he'd get on the road, but he just wants to be with the kid. Matthew stays all night, not that it'll change anything. Maybe it just puts off the feeling until he gets back on the highway.

"Gonna be in big trouble when I get home," says Matt.

"They give you any shit, tell 'em they'll have to deal with me."

"Hey trucker, you got any problem, you call me. Maybe I can help you forget him."

Right. Castor looks into Matt's boyish eyes, smiles for once.

Matt lights up, seeing his guy smiling at him. He's been emotionally beat up all his life. His family knows he's gay even though he denies it.

"You know I'm twice as fucking old as you are."

Matt's so happy with this guy. "Yeah. And also twice as fucking hot." He wishes he had more to share with Castor than his boring face and crappy life.

"Thanks. I'll try to call you sometime." Castor holds Matt's hand for a little, hugs him. Matt does that "kiss the mustache" thing, runs his fingers through it in a worshipful silence, then goodbye. The kid's a mess.

Off to Fayetteville, Bentonville, then Tulsa. What a crappy day of short hauls. When mom's in the ground, he's going west to Arizona. Or maybe California. For now, he tries to draw a metal cage over Ricky's beautiful stained eyes. Not to feel like such a fool. Drive, like you used to before all this emotion shit started. Tim did it. Brought emotion into his fucking life when there was no need for it. Damn it anyway, Tim's gonna be doggin' the doorstep when he gets back.

Like a storm clearing in his head, the clouds slowly pull back. Just a few puddles of sorrow left on the sidewalk. Maybe they'll dry up.

Maybe not. Maybe never. Never want to stop loving Ricky, no matter what. We'll keep a few scars.

The driving mentality finally clicks in. Feels better. No thought. Watch the trucks, the signs, herd the fresh apples on their way to Fayetteville. Castor takes them there. Without him, the whole town can't eat. Yeah, he's good for something.

CHAPTER 12

Tim's long cycle finally breaks when Castor comes home. God, he's just watching the clock like Time's coming to an end. That day Ricky came over really did him in. Castor never called. He doesn't know what happened between them. He called Ricky and Sonia, but Ricky said they weren't getting on well and he'd better not come by. "Was it Castor? I know you went there."

"Yeah, it's Castor. Sonia thinks he stole my wedding ring. Anything to get at him."

"I miss him."

Unspoken. *Yeah. Me too.*

As usual at the Williams's home, it's TV and cigarette night. Castor's lighting up one after the other. Tim's never seen him smoke so much before. He's afraid to say a word. Everyone's on edge. Just him and Castor with Mama and the cat, watching the news in the living room. Kurds, Iraqis, Israelis, Lithuanians. Estonians, South Africans, Armenians. Nicaraguans. "You'd think we weren't living in America," Emma says.

Pounding at the door. "Open," she yells.

Sonia storms in, mentally dragging Ricky by the ear. She's been boiling for days.

"Castor, goddammit, I want my rings back! Where are they?"

Castor's on the couch, drips into a drawl. "Damn, Mama, she just busts on in an' acts like she's still livin' here or something."

"Shore do."

"Stop that hoosier south Missouri shit. Give me the fucking rings or I'll report you for theft."

"Them's Ricky's rings," Mama says, barely looking up. "He'll have to do it."

"Mama!!"

"Don't you Mama me, little girl. I been Sonia-ing for the past five years, and I ain't heard nuthin' outta you. I don't know how you ever got too good for me after I brought you into this world."

"You know what's going on, don't you!" Sonia glares at her mother.

"Uh huh. Castor do, too."

"I don't," Tim says.

Ricky looks at Tim. Looks at Castor. "Don't say it, Castor."

"Yeah. You said it all Sunday, didn't you?"

"I want to know what's going on between you two," Sonia demands. "Why don't you just leave Ricky the fuck alone? Stop fucking with my husband and stay out of our lives."

Nothing to lose. Castor puts himself on auto pilot and lets go. "I love Ricky."

"What?"

"I love Ricky. And Ricky loves me. He's just too 'shamed to admit it."

Three little words. Three lives destroyed at once. Let's go for the record. Castor's leaning forward in the chair. Sonia and Ricky still standing up. Ricky's still near the door, lookin' like he wants to duck out.

"Ricky 'n' I been messing around. He fucks me. Okay? He sticks his cock up my ass. That what you wanna know? And then I shoot and rub it all over his fucking face. His eyes, his nose, his mus*tache*. And he sticks his tongue out and swallows it right off my fingers. And he likes it. He can't fuckin' get enough."

Ricky casts his eyes to the floor. Tim feels the blows of the hammer with each word Castor speaks.

Sonia whirls around. "It that true?"

"Yep," Ricky says. "Every word. 'Cept the swallowin' part."

"Ricky, he's my brother!"

"I know that. You're the one that forgot."

"You've had an affair with my brother! My fucking brother. I spend my night alone, and you're making love to my brother! I could just throw up."

"Yeah." Ricky's smiling. Just the levity of the thing is all. "Castor asked me to live with him, and I told him I was stickin' with you. Happy enough?"

"Happy? Happy?"

"Happy happy happy!" Ricky says. Doesn't know what to do. She slaps him. He slaps her back.

Back to Castor. "How could you do this to me?"

Castor's unleashed quite an atomic reaction here. Couldn't have been any better. "You ain't got nothin' to do with it," he says. "He's just my man. You're just that twister tie no one can get off the loaf."

Of course Tim's a bit forgotten. It's the *I love Ricky* that does him in. The cum on the mustache he can deal with, it's the love. The nightmare comes true. His jaw trembles. "Where does this leave me?"

"I guess this leaves you *out!*"

"What am I supposed to do?"

"I don't know. It ain't my problem."

"Castor, you were my whole life! I loved you."

154

Castor can't keep much back now. Finish the job. Let it out. "Yeah, I know. Man, you're always here. I told you I didn't want a fucking relationship. I told you the first goddamm night you came over I didn't want a relationship. You keep comin' and comin' and comin'—"

"I thought you liked it."

"I do like you, Timmee, but you drive me crazy. You want something I don't have to give you. Timmee, I don't love you, I just don't. We're too different. Why you didn't figure that out from day one I'll never know."

"You and Ricky are different as night and day."

Tim and Ricky exchange a quick glance. Silent agreement. Don't tell. Don't make it worse.

"You keep on trying to mess with me and change me," says Castor, "and I don't want to be any more than this mess I already am. Just cool out!"

Tim's dying inside. "What do you want me to do?" Quiet. He knows the answer.

"Why don't you just go on outta here! Give me one minute's worth of peace. You just can't make up a re-fucking-lationship here just because you want to!" Eyes to Ricky. "*Can* you?"

Tim's up now. Looking back at Castor. "I guess I won't see you anymore, then." Takes Sonia's hand, hugs her quick, takes Ricky's hand, rubs his face, then goes out the door.

Sonia turns back. "Tim!"

No answer. He's off the property in seconds.

"We've got to get him. I'm afraid for him in this state." She looks around, standing between Ricky and Castor. No matter what happens, they've done her in good. Nothing she can say or do can change it, make it better, make it go away. "Aren't you at least sorry?"

155

Ricky looks back. "No. Maybe a little. Maybe for a couple reasons."
Castor sees a break. One last chance. "Still here, if you want."
Ricky shakes his head.

"You'd steal your own sister's husband, wouldn't you?" Sonia asks.
"Looks like he ain't goin'."

"Well Ricky," she says, "I guess we have to go talk. And I guess we have to find Tim." Back to Castor. "Where are our rings?"

Silence. Thick and humid. "Back behind the dresser." Castor looks at the rug. "You'll have to push it back. I think they're all still there. I ain't moved it since Mama swept behind it in '85."

Ricky goes in there. Castor's not about to move. Ricky looks around. Recent memories assault him from all sides. Outside they hear the scraping of the dresser over the floor. Slowly, each ring back on his hand. *Back to life, back to reality.*

Back to the living room. Castor's looking at the floor. Never at Sonia. He can feel her presence. Always did her best to make him feel like garbage. Wonders why.

Ricky kneels down, kisses Castor on the lips. He may never be back. Doesn't know. *Goodbye.*

Castor doesn't respond. He can't.

Sonia shrieks. "Ricky!! Let's go!"

They leave, and silence settles slowly back to Bleeck Avenue. Mama doesn't know what to make of it all. She sighs and goes back to knitting. "I told Tim not to get involved with this family. Told him time and time again."

Sonia plans to call Ricky every name in the book, but she figures they'd better find Tim first. She puts her heartbreak on hold. He couldn't go too far. Look up on Ecoff, Manchester, Forest, Bruno, Waldemar, where is he? Stop in front of the apartment, up the steps. Sonia bangs on the door. "Timmee!"

When Dale comes out, she runs down the steps. "Have you seen Tim?"

"Nope, sorry." He sees something's wrong.

"Please, if you see him, don't let him alone. I can't stop right now."

She had Ricky drive all over Dogtown looking. No sign. He's lost. Might as well go home, she says.

So he turns up to Highway 40, and Sonia uses this as her license to start on him. Calls him everything she can think of. Calls Castor every-thing she can think of. *An affair I could maybe understand, but Castor? Leading on my brother. A man, in any event. Our whole marriage is a joke. He'd do anything to get at me.*

Castor's a good man. The only defense there is.

I thought at least you'd show me some respect. Sonia can't get it out of her head. Her Ricky. In bed with her brother. It keeps coming back to her. Ricky enjoying sex with her brother. Castor's graphic description. Ricky sticking up his tongue, licking Castor's cum out of his mustache.

Ricky bears up under it. Figures he deserves it, from her standpoint. No, she never did a thing wrong. Never. Never never never. She put up with his bad jokes, his treatment of her as a sex object, his blatant in-consideration for everyone in the entire world but himself, but now to sleep with Castor Williams and lie about it for how long? Two years?

Yep. Two years.

Finally, pulling onto Craig Road, onto Craig Court, into the jumble of apartments of people living sedate and elegant lives in near West County. Ricky's hand flies across the car and nabs Sonia in the face. He's had enough.

"That's the second time you hit me today."

"Do you want a divorce??"

No humor in that one. No time to think. "No."

Why the fuck not? "Then shut up!"

"Do *you?*" Sonia asks him back.

"I know what you must feel like."

"You didn't answer my question."

"I'm not going to," he says. "Not until I'm sure of what your answer is."

In the house, Ricky's pounding the shit out of the Chopin Nocturne. Sonia's going out for awhile. One of her accounting friends is going to hear a lot about Ricky. Still tied into that fucking family. Emma and Castor. Dad was smart to go away. They still manage to humiliate her. Still, always, still. No one could have thought of a deeper humiliation if they had a lifetime inside her head. She gets into her car and off she goes. Ricky's one light was his fidelity. Tries to get it out of her mind. She'd kiss him good morning after he'd been sleeping with her brother. Low class, unshaven, uncouth, uncultured, uneducated, just bring out the dictionary and go to the "un" section. *Christ, not even another woman.*

Tim takes a long route. Just a little bit north. He can't go home. He can't look at the keyboards and see all the songs he wrote for Castor. No. Got to go somewhere where all vestiges of Tim Dawson don't exist. Unknown to humankind. Leaves out bars, leaves out friends. Leaves out home.

Right north of Dogtown is Forest Park. Site of the 1904 World's Fair. The zoo, the art museum, the pavilion, the history museum. Long stretches of bike paths, woods, trees, open grass, picnic areas. Here and there little stone structures. Maybe decorative in their day, most are falling apart. Tim leans on one of these. How do you escape your own body?

Castor was his whole reason for being. His whole creative impetus now, his whole conversation, dedication, everything was built around Castor. The house of cards. Tim was afraid, but never believed it would happen. Castor loves Ricky. *Always loved Ricky. Never me. It was all a sham.*

Tim lays there, stares into the impending darkness. Doesn't want to cry. To cry would be to think about it. Hurts too much. Time to approach nirvana. Somehow. Just get totally numb. No feeling. Can't feel anything good. Life goes on—maybe not. It never works out, does it? *Castor could have me and he just doesn't want it. That's what's worse. At least Ricky has a reason. Castor doesn't. He just doesn't love me. That's all. I wish it didn't matter as much as it did. But too late for that.*

He thinks of a song. Can't come up with any words. Who'd want to hear it? Who'd want to share this much hurt? Maybe he could go back to Castor. Ricky's gone, and maybe he could have a chance. But it's not Ricky. It's him. *Castor doesn't love me.* Stevie Nicks never had it so bad. The last joke he ever thinks of.

Just knew it would happen. He could feel it. Why not turn away sooner? Because Castor was. Castor existed, and Tim needed it. Needed some man, some family, anyway, but mostly the man. To say, hey, it's okay. I will be here for you.

Thinks for a minute. He could go to Magnolia's and get five guys. He looks good enough. They've been waiting for weeks for Castor to dump his ass so they could go for it. No one there worth a damn. Just worth to flirt with for a minute, but no more. No one like Castor anywhere. They talked behind his back, saying it would never work and Tim was a fool. He never heard it, but he could feel it.

A Danish disco song goes through his head. Easy to hear. Meaningless syllables, don't know what they're saying, don't have to think about it.

Night comes, park curfew's at ten o'clock, but no one pays attention. Tim's alone on his rock foundation, hears some guys come up. Six guys. Six stupid, illiterate and troublesome young guys. *Get the fuck away from me.*

Khalid, Waldo, and Ronell are Black. Gary, Philip, and Jop are White. Integrated gang of kids, in St. Louis of all places. The Black kids wish they were White, the White kids wish they were Black. They don't like themselves, and they don't like each other for being the color they wish they were. Someone has to pay, and the guy on the rocks looks like a good start. A flashlight shines on Tim. On his t-shirt. Lesbian and Gay Pride 1985.

Khalid can even read. Barely. Makes out the words "lesbian and gay" and that's enough for him. "You a fag, motherfucker?"

Stupid kid. No answer.

Gary takes over. "Hey, motherfucker, he's talking to you. He asked if you were a fag."

Tim can't think straight. Just wants to be left alone. Just to hurt. It may never go away. "Go away," he says.

"Hey, this motherfucker won't answer my question." Khalid addresses his friends. "I think we got ourselves a faaag here."

Tim thinks to run, but has no energy. Six of them, one of him. Just looking for trouble, that's all. Just trying to blame someone else for the fact that they're illiterate assholes.

"Me and Waldo don't like faaaaags," Khalid informs Tim.

"Bet you wanna suck all six dicks," Philip laughs.

Guys are just looking for someone to beat up. White, Black, gay, straight, pretty random on their part. Gayness just an excuse. Tim can barely feel it. He's numbed. Castor hurt him worse than these punks. Castor's knife's sharper, his fists harder. Tim's blood more real. He never remembers feeling such pain. A gang tossing him around like a lost ship in a storm. Just hurting him for the hell of it. Just because they need something to do. A fist here, a knife there, made all the worse by the glee of his attackers. Sharp, searing blade-induced pain he knows only dying will stop; like the news of his family's car accident, it's that same pain only physical. A shriek just brings a punch to the mouth and "shut up, faggot." Now near the end, he will be humiliated one last time and go out on a wave of senseless hatred. No love. No friends. Just the impossibility of more metallic hurt than he knew was possible.

He feels dead anyway. Why not finish it off? Tries to send love. Send it to Castor, if Castor even wants it. If it can get through, maybe one more time. Think of Castor, maybe the pain will go away. No, that just hurts too.

Routine police check, two men in a squad car. Keep the park quiet. Lights up on Tim's way out. Five, six, how many? Runnem down. Look what's going on. They're beating that kid over there. Call in an ambulance.

Ronell gets away, Khalid and Waldo wind up in the back of a cop car in handcuffs. Khalid calls the cops motherfuckers. Everyone in Khalid's world is a motherfucker, but at least in this small gang he was respected as leader. Cops radio for help, some other cops pick up the white guys. They can beat an unarmed kid, but they cower in the face of a gun. Five out of six taken down. For now, that'll do.

Police see Tim lying unconscious by his rocks. Thankful he was put out of his misery. The only regret was that he didn't have enough time for it to set. Life always seemed so useless. He was always trying somehow to get somewhere, but it was never enough. Maybe this was just as well. Go with the rest of the family, in peace. No one has an easy ending. So many thoughts heading through Tim's head, all at once, all trying to make some sense out of his life before it's taken from him, useless death after a useless life. Twenty three years, all gone.

Cops check through his ID. *In case of emergency, contact Castor Williams, Bleeck Avenue; Sonia or Ricky Rutledge, Craig Ct.; Dale Terell, Waldemar.*

"Damn," the cop says. "He's got a fuckin' white pages in here."

Ricky gets the call. Hopes it's someone who can get him out of his mess. Someone who can help him out. *Tim Dawson? I know him. Sure, I'll be right there.* Leaves a note. Needs to. Whatever Sonia may be, Tim cared for her. She cared for him. God, he got her on that count, too. *What a way to live, setting everyone who loves you against each other.*

Speeds down Highway 40 to the emergency room at Barnes Hospital. See what's up with Tim. Stab wounds. Oh God, knives too? Beaten, bloody, bruised. *Where's that guy I took to Chicago just last week?* He can't see Tim yet. They're trying to save his life. Yeah, a group of hoodlums came by and beat the shit out of him. Just for the hell of it. Police still at the hospital for a little bit, hoping Tim might come around and they can get a statement, but they saw enough to have a case. Doctors say they don't know if Tim will come around. Ever.

Not much to do but keep him on machines, give him blood, stitches, and medication. At least he's not awake; he'd be in a lot of pain. Ricky wonders if somehow it's his fault. The whole Castor thing comes around to Ricky. No, it can't be. Castor could have kept Timmee. Didn't want to. Just an accident, a quirk of fate. They tried to find him, but they couldn't. He drove all around looking to make Sonia happy. Not that he's ever made her happy before.

She shows up and all is forgotten for now. *How's Tim? I got your note. Thank you.*

The thank you was unnecessary. Just an admission that Ricky might have a good quality somewhere. "They don't know."

"I wish we could have found him."

"Me too. I wish he'd have stayed."

"Well, after Castor—"

"Not now."

"You're right. Sorry."

"Is he gonna live?"

"I don't know."

"He was such a good friend." Finally it gets to her. Anger gives way to sorrow. Cloudburst, heavy dark rain. Tears. Poor Timmee. He had so much to give, and they've ruined him for no reason. For no reason.

"They got most of them."

"I hope they fry."

"Yeah. They don't know what they did. Just for fun."

Nowhere else to turn. She takes Ricky's hand. He looks in her eyes, she looks at him. Waterlogged electricity passes through. *Look what we've done to each other.* No more need be said. Ricky tries, Ricky feels what he hasn't felt in a long time. He feels home. "I guess no."

"No what?"

Quiet. Accepting. The first time in years he felt it. She accepted him. "Your question earlier. I guess no. Still."

"Yeah. I guess no."

"God, we've been so shitty to each other. Mostly me. Please forgive me."

So hard, so so hard. How? "I wonder if we can change," Sonia says.

Ricky looks deep. "I don't know. But it's what we got. And at least we got *something.*"

"Something. I guess maybe something is all we can hope for. Maybe we can make it into something good."

Eyes water, words are hard, best friend lies in the other room dying, something might as well be saved. "Maybe it's a start." A long hug there in the hallway, doctors and nurses looking on, walking by. Almost feels good. *Finally, she's here for me.*

Finally, he's here. For once. I can hold him and feel comfort. As much as I can feel, after all of it.

Ricky wonders if it's worth the hassle. To build on the legacy they've given each other. Wonders if she'll ever stop ragging at him. Wonders if someday he'll be back on Castor's doorstep. At least tonight, there is love. *Let's remember it. It may be all we ever get.*

Sonia calls Castor.

"What the fuck do you want now?" It's about midnight, maybe later. She never calls him.

"It's Tim, he's been beat up. I think you should come and see him. We're at Barnes. Emergency."

"Ain't my problem."

"Castor, he may die. This is no time for that."

"I told you it ain't my problem."

"Castor, please. He loved you."

"Well, ain't the shoe on backwards now." Sonia can hear the voice is strained. Nothing she can do. Sounds like he's very, very drunk. "Man, I got rid o' him. It ain't my responsibility anymore. He's gone outta my life."

"It happened because you threw him out. We'll come get you if you've been drinking. You could at least—"

"It didn't happen because I threw him out. It just happened." He's screaming at her. "I don't wanna hear no more about it." A little quieter, but definite.

CHAPTER 13

Driving again, back into the groove of how things were, before Ricky, before Tim, before all these people intruded into his rocklike existence. Castor searches around for a little photo of his car. Matt might find it entertaining. Maybe he's into cars. *Ricky really liked my car.*

Kind of feels a little better in a way, not wanting anybody, not having to worry about anybody. Tim made him feel so dumb, sometimes. Like his life was all wrong. Always wanting him to do this and that. Well, it wasn't *his* fault Tim went wandering around where he wasn't supposed to. Forest Park at night? You can't trust the whole world.

Castor saw something about it in the newspaper Monday. Even the police were outraged. Even if he was gay, this wasn't right. He was just sitting there doing nothing. Khalid made this stupid videotaped confession. He didn't have much choice. They caught him in the act. Denial wasn't working, and Khalid wasn't too smart, anyway.

"He was a fag, you know. It just seemed like something to do. That's what they do in those rap songs, you know." No emotion, no remorse, just something to do. Some of the other guys blamed Khalid for leading them into it. Maybe if anything, it would let the world know that a gay guy's life made a difference. Maybe. It's 1991, not 1951 after all.

Drive, run away from it. If Sonia doesn't call bearing any more bad news, maybe it will fade away. Tim'll go on living his pitiful little life and Sonia can have all she wants from whoever will give it to her. Typical

Sonia. It's always someone else's fault.

Matthew Tex shows up again at the truck stop. Black eye, bruises. No big deal, got into it with Trevor. "Last time I came home. They called me a fag, and we got into it. Family don't like me bein' gay."

"Sorry. You're a good man."

"Used to it. I socked him a good one, too."

"Here's a picture of my car. What do you think?"

"It's nice. Maybe I can ride in it someday."

"Maybe."

Castor doesn't want to be bothered with details of the Barlotti bustup. One fight a week is enough. He keeps thinking of Tim, looking into this broken young face. Perhaps he should have gone to see him. Tim was a friend, at least.

"I bet you'd like a nice back rub after driving in that truck all day."

Here we go. "Yeah, I bet I would."

Castor takes off his shirt, lays down in his little bed behind the cab. Matt likes seeing him like this. Matt's got cool small hands. It feels good, but just in the sense that it's a guy touching him. Nothing special, nothing like Ricky, like Tim, no feeling other than what's there. But Matt thinks the only way to cement a friendship is to do this. Let him go. *I want to rub your chest, Castor.* Of course.

At least he's ready to feel something, anyway. The driving isn't all that much of an escape, so maybe sex will work for a minute or two. A little better. Matt's not gonna stop there. *Shit, he's eighteen.* Castor figures he'll lay back and enjoy the kid's fascination with him. He's really not very good, definitely not much to look at, but what the heck, it takes his mind away for awhile. Matt's got this dumb smile like *Gosh, you're really gonna like me now,* so Castor keeps his eyes closed. Can't deal with it. Not another guy liking him, not now.

Matt gets the jeans off, get his mouth going on Castor, never tires, downs the seed with need and greed. He looks up at Castor and smiles. Stuff drippin' off his lip. *What is with you people? Tim too!* Everyone thinks they're going to live forever.

"Man, that was nice," Castor says, "but you know you shouldn't be doin' that."

"I know. But I trust you. This is really fun for me."

"Don't be stupid."

"I'm not stupid. I know what I like. And I know what kind of man you are. You're lonely, but you're good inside." Castor gives in, reaches over, puts his rough hewn truckin' hands on Matt and gets him off. Doesn't take long. Matt's been on edge, wanting this for a long time. He smiles, but it hurts his face.

"I just kind of wait for these days," Matt says. "We can get together, and it's almost like the other days don't matter."

"That's why I've been drivin' down here for the last ten years."

"I guess we need this, then, don't we?"

Castor just lays there, shakes his head. "Don't get started with me, kid. I don't need it."

Matthew gets a lump in his throat. His trucker calling him kid. "Wouldn't it be nice to know there's someone waitin' down here to take care of you after drivin' in a truck all day?"

Just the two of them, isolated from everything in a dark cool cab.

Matthew continues. "I really like you, Castor."

"I like you, too."

"This is all I have, man. I can't afford to move out, and I have nowhere else to go. Gay boy on the streets of Little Rock? Don't think that ever comes out good. I'm tired of runnin'. I tried. I came home that first time you picked me up, and it was all the same. I don't know how else to get out. Guess you can't keep me."

"I ain't savin' your life, kid." Barely recovered himself. Maybe not recovered, but there's always someone a little more desperate. Wants to tell Matt to go home. He can't deal with it. Can't deal with being the only good thing in somebody's life. Not again. *If I'm the only good thing—and look at me, garbage that I am.* "Look, you can hang out with me, but I'm not looking for any big emotional thing." Words, all too familiar, all too true. Wants Ricky back. Somehow he was so easy to love, so easy to commit to. The rest of the world is all trash. Why is Ricky picking someone who—never mind.

This time it's a full kiss on the lips. Matt wants the whole mustache. He doesn't understand how deep everything is, how old, how tired. He will in time.

But it makes Castor think a little, hope that Tim's okay. Maybe Castor serves some purpose to these young guys as some kind of loser hero. Aloof, quiet, never in one place for too long, never really going anywhere. Maybe Tim did need him for something, but it was so much, all the time. No, he didn't love Tim. Why should he feel bad about that? The truth is the truth. Truth sucks, but it's the way it goes. A little lesson he learned along the way. Tim would have to find out eventually.

But maybe it would make Tim feel a little better just if Castor came by to say hi. *I don't want a relationship, but I still care about you. Maybe we could get together now and then. Just don't stick to me so much.*

Phone call to the Rutledge place. Scary. Ricky'll wreck him, Sonia'll kill him. He can't blame her.

It's Sonia.

"Hey."

"Castor, what do you want?"

"How's Timmee?"

"He died. Monday. And we buried him Thursday." She's trying to be cold, but can't keep it in.

"Why didn't you tell me? I was here Monday."

"You didn't want to know, remember? You didn't want to be bothered."

"I wanted to see him again. I'm sorry." *For so many things.*

"We're all sorry. Castor, I don't wanna talk to you anymore. Ever." Hangs up.

Tim's death takes off like a rocket in the gay community, in the whole city, and a little across the country. A hate crime. *Forest Park isn't safe, what did I tell you?*

Just because he had on a gay/lesbian t-shirt, they had to kill him. Khalid opened his big mouth about rap music, so now everyone has a cause. Greggson Boggs leads the team. He hasn't seen Tim since that time in the shop, telling him Castor was no good for him, but he takes up the mantle. *Maybe something good will come out of it. Maybe straight people will see that it's not fair what they've been doing to us. Not fair to beat us and kill us just because we exist.*

Tim's picture is in the paper. Once again, he's famous because of death. So handsome, so talented, dead on account of a scumface like Khalid Watkins and his little gang. Khalid was a nothing. Never amounted to anything. Never will. Now he'll go to prison, and if Boggs gets his way, he'll die. Not that it will help. No one will miss him to begin with, and it won't bring anything back.

Chuck the DJ dedicates a Saturday night to Tim and plays all his songs over the loudspeakers at Magnolia's, everything Tim's given him over the last couple years. He even plays the bad ones, just something to remind people that Tim was trying. Everyone knew him. Everyone liked him, everyone wanted to be his friend. He was such a nice guy. Sweet, gentle, and we've been robbed. *Where's his girlfriend that came out with him? Too bad she can't be here for the tribute.*

Some guys get carried away. Some go beat up on straight guys just for the hell of it, just to show the other half how it feels. Black arm bands come out for awhile. *We've got to stick together. Wake up guys, it could have been any of us! Wake up!*

Doesn't matter. All the outrage in the world won't change things. An accident would have been better, not a knifing. Senseless.

The Dawsons go scurrying around, and they found his will. *The Tim, who?* relatives who faded out when his family got killed. *Look at him—he doesn't work and he's promiscuous. Who needs it? He's openly gay and it's embarrassing. Maybe he left us something.*

Having all that money made him think. He wasn't gonna give it to the aunts and uncles who didn't like him. It was a way to give to those he loved, even though hopefully decades down the road.

Ten thousand to Effort for Aids. Ten thousand to Dale Terrell. Fifty Thousand to Sonia and Ricky Rutledge, twenty-five each if they split. Tim wasn't sure, but he'd heard stories from both sides. Ricky gets all the studio equipment and keyboards. Ricky gets everything in the apartment if he wants it.

Ricky quits his job. *Never know what can happen. Might as well see what I can do with the studio. Never know how much time you have left. We'll make do with less.*

Castor sees Sonia on TV. Good friend of Tim's. The straight girl with the gay friend. She's crying. *How could this happen?* Look how it's affected her life. *Where's Ricky? Maybe he'll be on too, maybe I could see him one more time.*

Castor gets a call from a lawyer. *You get about a hundred fifty thousand dollars and a house in Rock Hill. We need to talk to you.* Okay. Castor hangs up the phone. He doesn't want a hundred fifty thousand dollars and a house in Rock Hill. He wants Tim. For all the shit that there was, maybe it was better than all this emptiness. It's harder to go back to his old ways than he thought. He keeps looking at his mother's sweater, but it triggers something. All the sorrow in the world was knitted into that sweater. He doesn't know if he can ever wear it.

Maybe the money can help his mom feel better, at least more comfortable. No sense in moving off of Bleeck Avenue after so long. Maybe he'll put Matt Barlotti up in Rock Hill. Maybe. No idea how so much money will change his life.

Phone rings again. It gets interminable. Maybe if he and Tim had something, it would be okay. He's got all this heroism now. *Tim's lover. How horrible you must feel.*

Right.

"Castor?"

"Yeah."

"Castor, this is Greggs Boggs."

"Who's that?"

"From the antique store. I liked your car."

"Yeah. What do you want?"

"I have a favor to ask you. I know this is going to be hard, but, maybe you could do something for us that might help a lot of people."

"What? I ain't never helped nobody no how. Just ask."

"We're all having trouble, you know. I know you're not part of the community, but we're having trouble saying goodbye. And we were hoping you might be able to say something. I wanted to have you talk on camera, just to say that—I don't know how to say this—we wanna show everybody that people who are gay are real people. And that we can be hurt and can love, and that we're not going to roll over while America rides over us roughshod. I know it's a hard time for you, but maybe this will help a lot of people see who we really are." Boggs is quiet, almost pleading, hoping for once to be seen as a man and not a statistic.

"I don't think so." Castor's in his room. No TV, no lights. *Damn Timmee, how could you...*

"It would mean a lot to us. Look," he explains. "Channel eleven has a spot for guest editorials and I think they're going to let us put something on. It's late at night, but it's something. They put on Tim Cusick...so the groundwork is there."

"I don't know who that is," Castor says. "Just some other guy named Tim to hunt down."

"He's a gay rights activist. He aggravates straight people but he makes things happen. And he's not afraid. They gave him a spot, so they're gonna be okay with it. I've already got it in motion." Greggs is so quiet, so different from last time. "And there's this radio show called *Lambda Reports.* It's on about six in the morning, but I talked to Charles Koehler, the host, and he'll play your tape. Maybe someone will accidently tune in at that hour," he tries to lighten it up.

"I don't think I need to go all over the TV tellin' people I'm gay and gettin' beat up. Ain't one enough? Look what just happened."

"That's the point. You're an everyday guy. It'd be a real good thing for you to do. Maybe make you feel a little better, anyway. Maybe for Tim. Maybe he'd feel you really loved him."

Castor haltingly tells Greggs more than he wants to, as he wonders how responsible he is. "I told him to get lost right before he died. He ran out of the house because I told him I didn't wanna see him anymore. We looked...well my sister looked...and she couldn't find him. So someone else found him. Everyone wishes things were different. We weren't as close as he kept saying. And everybody tries to make me feel bad about it. I had to end it, you know. I mean, I just had to, and my sister thinks I've killed him because of it. It's not true...and..." Tired of defending himself, just about to hang up. He could never express himself, and now the whole city wants to see him stumble over simple words.

"Castor, please. It would really help. Tim was loved by a lot of people. Please."

That last *please* turned his heart. "I don't know what to say."

"I don't either, but I'll try."

Emma comes to his door almost unheard, quite a feat seeing how hard it is for her to get around. "I don't like to listen in on your phone calls, and I don't like to mingle in your affairs," she says to him.

"But here you are, listening and mingling," Castor says.

"You've always been good to me, Castor," says Mom. "At the expense of your own happiness, and I know that."

"What's that matter with all this?" Castor feels bad having a private discussion in front of what's soon to be a TV journalist, even if he's just on the phone.

"Someone died as a result of having a fight in this house. Someone who loved you as much as I do. He was beaten and stabbed to death, and you can be sure his last thoughts were of you."

"It isn't because of me!" Castor gets louder than intended.

"It isn't," Emma says quietly. "But it is. So if you can't do it for him, do it for me. It's okay. Your father didn't want to hear what I had to say either when he was your age." Emma turns back from whence she came.

Castor is quiet, and he knows Greggs won't break this silence. He tries to wait it out, hoping Boggs will just hang up, but instead they

174

both just breathe quietly into the phone. Castor wants to go along with it at this point, but he doesn't want anyone to know. At least he has Emma to blame now. "Okay, if Mom says so," he says. "Gotta listen to my mom."

"I can write something. You can just read it. We have the tele-prompter. I'll just come to your house with a cameraman and we'll do it there. I'm not trying to use you, I hope you understand. It's just been hard."

Greggs sounds too convincing. Too sincere. None of the cockiness from the Emporium. *Maybe we'll try. Maybe it's a way to say goodbye myself.* Castor's so sick of these damn tears, dripping off his face for all eternity. Maybe it will make it all go away. Put an end to it.

Next day, Greggs come by. Fascinated with the house. All so old, but so new. "Bought it all new?"

"Back in 1955," Mama says.

Right before they had me and ran out of money, Castor thinks.

"See this chandelier? This lamp? We've always had it."

"It's a very nice house, Mrs. Williams. Castor, this is my lover. Ron. He'll just film you. Here's something I wrote. Only about three minutes is all. We want to get it on the news while it's still out there."

Castor reads through it. "It's not all true."

"Is it good enough? You can change it. You can say whatever you want. We really appreciate this."

Castor's sitting on the bed, half a cigarette burning by his side. Looks past the camera into the mirror.

Ron must really love Greggson, he's so much better looking. Yeah, Tim really loved me. He was so much better looking. Doesn't matter, really.

It's all set up. "Ready when you are."

Castor looks over at the teleprompter screen. Words roll past him. *Look into the camera. It doesn't have to be exact, just some ideas, is all. Look in the monitor.* It's Castor up against a bare wall. Looks like he's nowhere. Small picture in black and white. Cigarette smoke rolls up one side.

"My name is Castor Williams. I'm a truck driver—go from here to Little Rock and around the south, southwest. It's a truck. It goes where I go. You all probably heard of Tim Dawson, how he got beat up and killed because someone found him wearing a gay pride t-shirt in Forest Park. Tim was my boyfriend, my... lover... for the few months before he died. I just guess I'm here to wonder if maybe all you people out there think that because we're gay that we don't have hearts, that we can't feel for each other, that maybe our lives don't matter. That's what Khalid Watkins thought, that Tim's life didn't matter. Just because Tim loved a man.

"Tim was very gentle, very attractive, very talented. He was a musician. He was working on an album. Had a few good songs done already. He needed his friends because he had no family of his own. They were all killed in a car crash a couple years ago. I was his family. Me, and my sister, Sonia. She loved Tim, and she was straight. And her husband, Ricky, loved Tim...and he was...straight.

"It wasn't so much what he was, it was who he was..." Tears start again, Castor can see in the mirror. Stops for a minute. "Can't do this anymore..." Greggson motions gently to go on, *we're almost finished.*

Deep breath, *for effect, look at him, he's crying. Maybe we were wrong about him all along.*

Castor speaks in an alien language, words in ways he's never used them. "The gay community in St. Louis and the rest of the country isn't going to roll over and play dead any longer. We can't afford it. This is an appeal to all of you. Look at us, see us as people, not the enemy. We are out there with you and want to give all we can. We don't deserve to be called The United States of America until everyone is allowed to be a part of it. Until everyone is truly free." Looks up at the screen, silent for awhile, trying to focus his eyes, get a little strength back. Picks up the cigarette—no, never mind. In the monitor smoke curls up beside his half-curly hair.

"Tim never had his chance. We parted on some harsh words, my harsh words, and now I can never tell him how much he means to me... how much I cared for him, how much I—" Stop for a minute. "Fuck you Greggson, for making me do this!" Tears faster, why is this affecting him so much? *Thought Tim didn't matter. Thought so. He'll never be back now.*

"See, I really loved Timmee." Hard breath, one more to go, one more and it's all over. Finally, all over. "I really loved Timmee, and I don't know what I'm going to do without him."

Fade to black.

EPILOGUE

It's a few months later, and Castor's going through the mail. About once a week he'll bother to pick out the bills and scrawl out a few checks, but one letter sticks out funny. "Look Mama, they're takin' our house."

"Castor, you're trying to put me in an early grave."

"No, they're takin' it. Gonna put up a shopping mall in 1992. Bleeck Avenue's going under the wrecking ball."

"All of it? Just what we need here is more shopping."

"All of it. Whole bunch of streets." He's got a letter in his hand from the City of St. Louis or some such official authority as could demolish the house for the betterment of others. He reads a bit more. "We're getting compensation."

"Oh," Emma says. Castor sees she's processing this unexpected turn of events. "Funny, every time something bad happens we make money."

A hundred fifty thousand dollars and a house in Rock Hill.

"Better call them Rock Hill tenants and tell 'em times up," Emma says with a shrug.

"I guess." Castor's been in a fog, living much like before. Doesn't really think about how he's got a bulging bank account and a new place to live. Even after taxes, he has a load of money to his name like he's never seen before. It almost makes trucking an option rather than a necessity, but not quite.

"It's a blessing to get out of this place," Emma says. "You can just put me in a home and live in your truck," she chuckles.

"Don't think I haven't thought it." He smiles. But he takes a quick dart into the future, and moving to Tim's house is the easiest solution he can think of. "Yeah, okay. Where else we gonna go?"

Emma looks around at furniture that's been part of the house for so long it's like it was welded in place. "You call up that fat man and tell him to come get all this. We'll start over, you and me. Whatever time I got left."

"Me too. Too much time left."

"You got plenty more time than I do, so you might as well make use of it. And you got that Southern kid comin' around. So …"

"Just tryin' to make it all go away."

Some folks in the area put up a token fight against the shopping center, but the Williams family gives in without a squabble. They got money, they got a house. Sometimes Castor remembers the guy who made it all possible, but he tries not to.

Castor brings up Matthew Tex before his family shoots him. He's leery of living with a lovestruck beat up teenager, but he lays down some rules. "Look, this ain't no relationship or nothing like that. But you can live here. You can take care of Mama while I get in my truck and drive to California. Then I'm drivin' to Maine from there. And when I come back I'll be happy to see you. Plenty of places to get a job on Manchester."

Matt settles in like the dog coming to a new family out of the rescue shelter. Castor finally gets to drive past Fayetteville. He's out in Sacramento, in Truckee, Reno, Salt Lake City, each time thinking he'll reach into his bank account, get a place, and keep quiet about it. Call up Ricky Rutledge and say come on out and let's just be here. Each trip though, he comes home and holds Matt just a little closer. He can't bring himself to call Ricky. He tries. He dials three or four numbers and can't make himself finish. Anyway, Ricky knows where he lives.

Oh. No, not any more.

* *
*

Sonia tries for normalcy, but it's a long time before she can let herself make love with a man who was satisfying himself with her brother. Ricky doesn't even bring up making love, having sex, or whatever other colloquialism he used to use for it. They have to start as friends and see if passion will come back the way it did the first time, though they had nearly knifed it to death. Sonia realizes what she needs to know if she's going to stay with him, and she spends weeks trying to phrase the question.

"Ricky," she says, "I'm just going to say it. If you'd rather be with a man, there's no point in us staying together, so you need to be honest about it and let me know."

"I haven't talked to Castor since that night. Look, it was something I tried. I'm sorry."

"It was something you tried that was more important than our marriage."

"I know," Ricky says. "I still don't know how you'll ever forgive me. Or why you should."

"You think about it," she says. "I do love you." She kisses him, but she isn't sure if she's kissing her husband or her ex.

Ricky's been afraid to contact Castor. Even though he knows he can, he knows he shouldn't. If Tim's death does anything to Ricky, it brings home how he's used his good looks to manipulate everyone and everything around him and how it stunted his growth. Now seeing those looks in the mirror just makes him sad. He can't imagine he'll get any kind of good welcome from Castor, or worse, Castor's mother, but he's got to see him again to see how it makes him feel. On a gut level, on a deep heart-fluttering emotional level, how does it make him feel?

He gets in the car, cranks up a CD of Haydn's Symphony #47 in G major, and takes the drive down Manchester to Bleeck Avenue, but Bleeck's not there anymore. Just a cleared-out lot with signs promising a better future. K-Mart! Phar-Mor! Builder's Square! All coming soon and what a wonderful world it's going to be. He pulls up Waldemar Avenue in Dogtown and turns around. Oh, yeah, Tim lived here.

Comes home and Sonia's watching TV. "I was taking a client to O'Connell's for a burger," he says. "Your ma's house ain't there anymore. You know where they went?"

"I don't talk to those people."

Ricky weighs being a star in gay bar culture versus spending his life with an occasionally loving, always attractive but lately unhappy woman. Or a third choice, which is neither. He can't make up his mind, so he waits for Sonia to make up hers.

Sonia waits for Ricky to make up his, and their inertia keeps them together.

Finally, more through negotiation than romance, they agree to make love. "Either we're married or we're not," he argues. "What's it gonna hurt?"

She smiles, and he's happy to see it. "You always know just what to say."

Dale Terrell leaves his apartment in Waldemar and moves in with Darnell, who's got himself a small house in nearby Richmond Heights. For a while, Dale has unwanted fame as Tim's best friend, as the gay guy who lived downstairs from the gay guy who got beat to death. He's happy with his life, but sometimes he wonders what might have been different if one day when he made that trip upstairs he'd have told Tim how there was more than a casual visit on his mind. Sometimes at home, he puts Tim's music into a cassette player and dances to their friendship.

*
 * *

Tim's songs spend a few weeks on the charts at Magnolia's, then slowly drop away.